~~~~~~~~~~

MALIGN FORTUNE

~~~~~~~~~~~~~~~~~~~

The Seacastle Mysteries
Book 9

PJ Skinner

ISBN 978-1-913224-59-2

Copyright 2025 Parkin Press

Cover design by Mariah Sinclair

Dedicated to Una Willers and Sonja Charters who have helped me as beta readers since the beginning of this series. Both of them go above and beyond for me. My books wouldn't be the same without their careful revisions, and I am galvanised by their cheerful support.

Ladies, you are marvellous, and I truly appreciate you both.

Discover other titles by PJ Skinner

The Seacastle Mysteries

Deadly Return (Seacastle Mysteries Book 1)

Eternal Forest (Seacastle Mysteries Book 2)

Fatal Tribute (Seacastle Mysteries Book 3)

Toxic Vows (Seacastle Mysteries Book 4)

Mortal Vintage (Seacastle Mysteries Book 5)

Last Orders (Seacastle Mysteries Book 6)

Grave Reality (Seacastle Mysteries Book 7)

Lethal Secret (Seacastle Mysteries Book 8)

Poison Politics (Seacastle Mysteries Book 10

Purrfect Crime (A Christmas Mystery novella)

Mortal Mission A Mars Murder Mystery written
as Pip Skinner

Green Family Saga (written as Kate Foley)
Rebel Green (Book 1)
Africa Green (Book 2)
Fighting Green (Book 3)

The Sam Harris Adventure Series
(written as PJ Skinner)

Fool's Gold (Book 1)

Hitler's Finger (Book 2)

The Star of Simbako (Book 3)

The Pink Elephants (Book 4)

The Bonita Protocol (Book 5)

Digging Deeper (Book 6)

Concrete Jungle (Book 7)

Sam Harris Adventure Box Set Book 2-4

Sam Harris Adventure Box Set Book 5-7

Sam Harris Adventure Box Set Books 2-7

Also available as AI narrated audiobooks on YouTube
and from my website

Go to the PJ Skinner website for more info and to
purchase paperbacks directly from the author:
https://www.pjskinner.com

Chapter 1

Rain should be compulsory at funerals. Bright sunshine streamed out of the Seacastle sky, feeling like an unwelcome jovial attendee intruding on the sadness of Sarah Barrow's funeral. The small parish church where we were gathered shrank under the blinding midday sun, which sucked the colour out of the vegetation and bleached the cobbles in the courtyard. The combination of bright sunlight and black clothes did no one any favours. It emphasised the pinched faces creased with sorrow and dried our tears into salt deposits on our puffy cheeks. I found my dear friend Roz Murray in the centre of the hive of murmuring mourners and whispered my heartfelt condolences for the death of her mother. She barely acknowledged me, lost in the fog of grief. Her husband, Ed, shrugged at me and shook my partner Harry Fletcher's hand.

'She's taken it very hard,' he said to me. 'She'll need you more than ever.'

We stood in the crowd for a while, greeting fellow mourners and exchanging comments on the demise of Sarah Barrow, mother of Roz and well-known local gossip. Roz had inherited the habit, so we had to be cautious about telling her anything we didn't want broadcast all over Seacastle. She wasn't in the mood for chatter now. Her hunched posture emitted waves of misery, which affected everyone around her. The heat of the day made me feel nauseous, and I darted into the cool embrace of the small church as soon as I could navigate my way through the throng. Harry followed me indoors, bemused by my haste to enter it.

'I'm not sure we should be in here yet,' he whispered. 'Don't they have some sort of seating plan?'

'Sorry, sweetheart. I couldn't bear it out there. My black wool suit absorbs sunlight like a solar panel. I was melting like the Wicked Witch of the West.'

I pointed to a large bead of sweat, which had run down my nose and dallied with the tip.

'Didn't she melt in the rain? I thought you were crying.'

'I didn't know Roz's mother well enough to be sad. I met her a few times when we were young, but Ed called her the Kraken.'

'All men think their mothers-in-law are Krakens. Did Roz have a close relationship with her mother?'

'Not for years. Sarah disowned Roz after she married Ed. They had been attempting a reconciliation recently, but I'm not sure how that went. Roz hasn't talked about it.'

'Poor old Roz. She had no time to prepare herself for this either.'

'I'm not sure anyone can prepare for losing a parent.'

'I wish my mum were alive. I don't think I ever had an argument with her.'

'My mother's obsession with the Squander Bug and eating mouldy food from the fridge used to worry more than annoy me.'

'All that generation had to tolerate food rationing after the Second World War. My mother always told me she hadn't eaten a banana until the fifties.'

'That's what she told you,' I said, making him guffaw.

The church echoed with the unfamiliar sound.

'I'm pretty sure that's blasphemy of some sort, casting aspersions on my dear departed mum.'

'I'm sorry. Funerals always bring out my rude side. I think it's a reaction to the finality of it all.'

'Are you sure?'

'Am I sure of what?'

'That death is final?'

'Quite sure. Although I'm convinced heaven is actually the knowledge that people you loved and who loved you remember you for years after you've gone.'

'And hell?'

'When people forget you, as if you never existed.'

'I think I preferred the rude jokes.'

The door creaked open behind us, and the black-clad mourners flooded inside and occupied the benches like an oil leak on a corrugated floor. Roz had requested that we only wear black, as her mother had specifically asked for it. I felt the weight of Ghita Chowdhury's thigh squeezed up against mine as she sought comfort amongst the misery. She and I and Roz were best friends, and she found it hard to deal with Roz's loss.

Roz may not have got on well with her mother, but it seemed everyone else did. I noticed a flash of colour near the back of the church. Miles Quirk, a local antique dealer, lurked behind the pillars, a bright cravat at his throat. He couldn't resist breaking with convention. I wondered how he knew Roz's mother. Knowing him, he'd be up for a gossip at the wake which Roz had asked me to hold at the Vintage, the café above my second-hand furniture shop, Second Home. Roz and Ghita both helped me at the shop on days when I needed them or they were not busy elsewhere. Ghita had baked all week to provide the food for the mourners, and my son Mouse had offered to man the coffee machine. We had bought cheap filter coffeepots and teapots from the nearby Cat's Protection charity shop to make serving easier. I intended to give them back after the wake.

No-one could have accused the vicar of dawdling through the service. I caught him checking his watch as Sarah's sister clung to the lectern, forcing out happy memories of her sibling.

'Probably wants to watch Man United play Liverpool,' said Harry, when I told him.

The mourners bowed their heads as the ushers wheeled the coffin past the oak benches. One wheel squeaked loudly, making me wince.

'That trolley needs some WD40,' said Harry, practical as ever.

Roz shuffled past us without looking up. She clutched her phone in her hand; her knuckles white.

'She won't put it down,' whispered Ghita. 'She listens to a recording of her mother's voice over and over. I hope she's going to be okay.'

I remembered how I had felt when my mother died. Orphaned and abandoned, despite being in my thirties. I wished she had met Harry and seen how happy

I became after she died. I couldn't believe how much my life had changed over several short years. Harry tugged my arm.

'Are you going to the burial?'

'Can you represent us, darling? I've got to brew pots of tea and coffee for the wake.'

'Sure, Roz won't mind. She looks past caring at this stage. We need to keep an eye on her.'

I kissed his cheek.

'Don't be long.'

I headed for Second Home, my head full of memories. Sarah Barrow had not played a large part in my childhood. She was not one of those mothers who ran an open house for their children's friends. Roz did not romanticise their relationship either. They simply didn't get on when Roz was little, a gap that grew wider after Roz hit her teenage years. I never got the impression she treated Roz badly, but she seemed oddly indifferent to her. I was not my mother's favourite either, but she never ignored me. At least I had time to say goodbye on my terms, and was not left with things unsaid like Roz.

I parked on a side street off the High Street and trotted to my shop door. The bulk of the catering had already been done, and my primary task consisted of funnelling boiling water into the tea and coffee pots. I distributed the tea and coffee evenly between the two floors. The Vintage Café on the first floor had more formal seating than the downstairs part of Second Home, but when you sell furniture, you never lack chairs and tables for people to sit at. Harry and Mouse had pushed the wardrobes and dressers into the back storage room and made a central space for people to stand in. I removed the price labels from all the furniture, taking photographs of each piece so I remembered the prices. When I had finished getting ready, I sat at the counter, ready to discourage any customers who ignored the polite notice on the door about the wake and tried to browse my shop instead.

Not long afterwards, the first mourners arrived at Second Home. They congregated in the social space, discussing the funeral in hushed whispers. I passed among them, pouring tea and coffee and offering bite sized snacks, which showcased Ghita's culinary talents. I noticed Miles Quirk poking around in the storeroom and checking out my stock. There was no point in complaining. He may have been a pain, but he also bought a lot from me without bartering me down. Instead, I wagged my finger at him, and he gave me a wicked grin. Roz came in on Ed's arm, and he helped her upstairs, trailing a crowd of mourners like a murmuration of misery. I girded my loins for a long afternoon.

Chapter 2

At the shop the next morning, Harry and Mouse helped me to unload the van of the haul garnered from our latest house clearance, before heading off to London with the items I wouldn't be able to sell. Mouse's return from University was the best thing about May. He is my ex-husband George's son from his first marriage, which ended soon after it started. His real name is Andrew, but he prefers Mouse. I love Mouse as my own, even though we are not blood relatives. He moved in with me after George bought me the Grotty Hovel and never left. He's ferociously bright and has a reputation as a hacker. George persuaded him to study forensic computing at Portsmouth to put his skills to good use. Since George is a detective inspector in the local police force, he may have had an ulterior motive.

Almost as soon as they left for London, the skies opened, and a heavy downpour fell on the town. The teeming rain poured down onto the High Street in wet sheets, driving away any prospective customers. I shrugged at the deluge and went upstairs to make myself a latte and scrounge a piece of cake left over from the funeral. I noticed some of Ghita's delicious almond biscuits hiding under a napkin and rubbed my hands together in anticipation. They melted in your mouth if you didn't munch them up immediately. I had forgotten to ask her to make some lemon ones too. The problem with Ghita's cakes was how moreish they were. I had to remind myself they cost money, and I had to sell them, not gobble them up like a hungry seagull.

I sat in the window and looked out at the water teeming through the street in the gutters and disappearing down into the drains. Pieces of rubbish soon blocked the grids, driving the water further down the street. Then, in the distance, a large pink and purple umbrella fought its way towards the shop. I jumped up and ran to open the door for Ghita who wore a bright pink raincoat and short grey wellington boots with mouse ears on them. She came inside dripping onto the floor, but she was bone dry underneath her raincoat.

'I had to walk upstream against the current,' she said. 'I felt as if I were a spawning salmon.'

'You looked like one, dressed in pink and grey. You're lucky you didn't get eaten by a bear.'

She smiled, but it didn't wipe the worry from her face.

'Have you heard from Roz?' she asked.

'No, I don't think she's in the mood for chatting after the funeral.'

'Of course. I should know that. I'm worried about her.'

'She'll be all right. It's hard to lose a parent. It takes time to adjust.'

Ghita shifted from foot to foot.

'Um, she's behaving weirdly.'

'Weirdly? Roz? Is that unusual?'

'I'm serious. She's got this recording of her mother speaking on her telephone, and she listens to it obsessively.'

'I saw her gripping her phone during the funeral. Maybe it brings her comfort to hear her mother's voice?'

'But that's not all. She's, she's…'

'She's what?'

'She's visiting a medium.'

'Oh, well, some people believe in that sort of thing. You know Roz. She dabbled in witchcraft and crystals. It's hardly surprising she would trust a person like that. It can't do any harm.'

'How can you say that? The medium charges her two hundred pounds a visit. Roz can't afford that.'

'Oh, that's steep. Is this medium any good?'

'He's famous.'

'What's his name?'

'Vivian Blackwood.'

'I've never heard of him.'

'Of course you have. He's been on BBC Breakfast.'

The BBC could do no wrong. As far as Ghita was concerned, anyone who appeared on BBC Breakfast had earned the right to be categorised as famous.

'What does he look like?'

'Sort of dreamy, really. I couldn't concentrate on his comments as I got distracted by his jawline.'

Ghita was as shallow as a puddle. She only fell for nasty men with pretty packaging, which meant she remained single despite all her efforts to find a 'nice man'. She hung out most of the time with Rohan and Kieron, the lovely owners of the Surfusion restaurant across the road. They let her use their kitchen to cook her wonderful cakes, and in return she helped them with the invention of new dishes and filled in as a cook when they were shorthanded. Unfortunately, they were a couple, so her love went unrequited in that case too.

'I'll talk to her, I promise. Meanwhile, would you like to help me polish the new stock?'

'Sorry, I'm due at the Surfusion. Rohan needs help in conjuring up the summer menu.'

'Do you want to take them some cake? There are tons left from the wake.'

'No thanks. They're both on a weird cabbage diet at the moment. I have to pretend I don't notice all the farting.'

I wrinkled up my nose at the thought.

'Are you sure you wouldn't prefer to buff my furniture?'

'I can't let them down. See you later.'

I watched her splosh her way across the road; a round, pink figure under an enormous umbrella. The door of the Surfusion opened, and Rohan pulled her inside, letting down her umbrella and shaking it onto the pavement. He caught sight of me watching and gave me a cheery wave. I waved back and then returned to my polishing. I have to admit, Roz's obsession with the medium struck me as odd despite my justifying it to Ghita. The death of her mother had discombobulated her.

Before I had long to ponder this, Roz herself came into the shop, looking haggard and unkempt. Her mop of blonde curls hung lank around her face, and she wore an old cardigan with more holes than buttons. She attempted a smile, and I gave her a warm hug, which she failed to reciprocate. Her arms flopped back to her sides while I was still locked in.

'Do you want a coffee?' I said. 'There are still plenty of cakes left upstairs.'

Her eyes widened. 'Cakes? Who left them there?'

'From the wake, I meant.'

'Oh.'

Such a small sound. She seemed so diminished I felt worried. She had the nickname Foghorn for good reason, and this odd reaction did not seem like her at all. It was as if she had been buried along with her mother.

I took her by the arm.

'Come on then. Let's go upstairs.'

She let me lead her up without resisting. I wondered if the doctors had prescribed her some sort of sedative or antidepressant to help her get through the grief. It didn't seem likely. Roz never went to a medical doctor if she could help it. She frequented herbalists and acupuncturists and chiropractors, but she had a peculiar fear of chemicals. I never told her she was made of chemicals, just like everything else on earth. I didn't want to have an argument, and Roz knew how to defend her corner.

We sipped our coffees in silence until I dragged up the courage to question her about her visits to see Vivian Blackwood. She could be touchy if she felt judged. Ghita often bantered with Roz, but she could never face a confrontation. She told me things she wanted to discuss with Roz and let me face the music on my own. Since

Ghita had left me with the responsibility of finding out the truth, I couldn't resist dropping her in it.

'Ghita tells me you went to see a medium.'

'Typical. You can't do anything in this town without people gossiping about you.'

Since she had occupied the number one spot on Top of the Gossips of Seacastle for many years, this struck me as disingenuous, to say the least. I did not rise to the bait.

'I think she was concerned.'

'Concerned? I don't know why. The man's a legend. He's put me in contact with my mother and made me feel a hundred times better.'

Her face lit up for a moment, and her eyes blazed with the light of fanaticism. It startled me no end. I wondered if Ed knew what Roz was up to.

'Really? That's amazing. He's got quite a reputation. I'd love to meet him if you are going again.'

'I'm going to a seance at his flat tomorrow. You can come. But if you make one rude comment about Vivian or the seance, you'll have to leave.'

'Would I dare?'

Chapter 3

Before visiting Vivian Blackwood, I intended to enlist the help of Mouse to do some research into his credentials. However, Mouse had gone to the pub with Goose and his other friends, and I knew better than to expect an early return. Harry drew his eyebrows together when I told him what I had planned.

'A medium? Like Mystic Meg?'

'I'm not sure Mystic Meg claimed to be a genuine medium. She did a spot on the National Lottery draw for years.'

'She had a string of racehorses too. One of my cousins used to bet on her horses any time they raced. He lost a fortune.'

'Anyway, not like her. Although he has appeared on television.'

'Is he the real thing?'

'I shouldn't think so. Most mediums are people readers. I expect he picks up cues as he gets to know his clients.'

'But why is Roz seeing him? Does she believe in that sort of thing?'

'She used to be into witchcraft and all that, so it's not beyond the realm of possibility.'

'She's always been away with the fairies. I suppose it's not much of a stretch to communicate with spirits instead.'

'We'll soon find out, I suppose.'

'I'm not bad at predicting the future, you know.'

'Really?'

'I can see a tikka masala with poppadums being brought to you by a handsome man in about half an hour.'

'Now that's the sort of prediction I appreciate.'

The next morning, I fed Hades and Harry, in that order, before setting off to Pirate's Harbour to pick up Roz. She and Ed did not own a car, so she cycled around Seacastle, balancing improbable amounts of shopping on her handlebars and in her saddlebags. As I drove down to the harbour, I spotted her sitting on a bench near the stone pier, her fair, curly hair flattened by the breeze. She still wore black, but her skirt had a wide lace border, and her top was decorated with sequins. The resulting outfit was more Madonna than Scottish Widows, which gave me hope she might be recovering a little from her loss.

I gave the horn a light toot, and she turned to face me. Her cheeks were shiny with tears, but a bright smile lit up her face. She came over to the Mini and jumped in.

'I'm so glad you're coming with me,' she said. 'He's unlike anyone I've ever met before. You'll be blown away by his insights and his ability to communicate with the spirit world.'

'I promise to suspend my disbelief and keep an open mind.'

To my surprise, Vivian did not live in a cottage with wisteria and ivy growing on the walls, but on the seventh floor of one of the tower blocks on Seacastle's seafront. We rode up in a lift under the scrutiny of a CCTV camera. I noticed the red light blinking as it monitored the comings and goings of the building's residents. I wondered if that accounted for the working lift and well-maintained appearance of the building. Big Brother watching would deter the local rough element from entering. That and the loud classical music piped into the lobby and lifts. Vivaldi's Four Seasons can grate on the ear when it's ubiquitous, especially if you prefer rap.

We were greeted outside the flat by a young woman whose face and arms were a riot of colourful tattoos. She had a nose ring, ears with multiple piercings and when she spoke, a tongue stud flashed at me.

'Can you wait outside Mrs Murray? Vivian is not yet ready to communicate with the bereaved.'

She shut the door again and left us standing there.

'Who was that?' I asked.

'Titania Grafton. She's Mr Blackwood's assistant.'

Titania? I wondered if she had chosen that name for herself. Perhaps she didn't know who Titania was. I looked around the concrete stairwell. Four wooden chairs sat outside the door of the flat, placed without ceremony on a cement floor. We sat beside each other on two of them and waited in silence, listening to the sounds echoing up the stairwell from the floors below us. Roz took out her phone and listened to something, with an expression of deep sadness on her face. I waited for her to explain, but she seemed oblivious of my sitting beside her. I shut my eyes for a minute and soon dozed off.

A sharp bang woke me up with a start. I looked around to see an old lady wearing an elaborate kaftan and a silk turban coming around the stairwell towards us. Had she come from one of the flats? Before I could ask her a question, several more people exited the lift. They shook hands with Roz and introduced themselves, all except the old lady who ignored me.

'Emily Carradine, schoolteacher. Retired now. Hoping to speak to my baby.'

'Natalee Hedges, beautician. Missing my sister.'

'Raven Huxley, influencer. Here to interview Mr Blackwood.'

A mixed bag. All with different reasons to be there. No one mentioned auras or ectoplasm while we waited, which I found a little disappointing. I wanted to ask questions, but Roz elbowed me hard any time I seemed about to speak. I gave up. Titania reappeared, waving a kitchen mixing bowl under our noses.

'Phones, please.'

Roz and the other participants dropped theirs in without a murmur. I searched through my handbag and came up empty-handed.

'I don't have it with me,' I said, patting my pockets.

'Vivian doesn't like telephones in the communing room. They interfere with the spirit world.'

'I just told you I haven't got it with me. I must have left it in the car.'

Incomprehension made her blink several times. She belonged to the generation who could not understand how anyone could be anywhere without their mobile telephone. I opened my handbag and showed her the contents. She shook her head.

'He won't take you as a client if you don't have a mobile.'

'I have one that got left in the car. I'm here to support my friend, and I am hoping to hear from my brother.'

She rubbed her nose and pouted.

'He won't mind, Titania,' said Roz. 'He told me to bring a friend with me if I wanted to.'

We followed her inside. The interior of the flat didn't disappoint. I could hear Harry's voice in my head. 'It's got more quartz than Crystal Palace'. The anteroom curtains were made of heavy velvet, blocking natural light from entering the room. The only lighting came from the table lamps covered in pink gauze.

Just then, the doorbell rang, and Titania tutted and swore under her breath. She opened the door, and a large, bald man pushed his way in, his face red with fury. She blocked his way and fixed him with an intense stare.

'You're not welcome here,' she said, holding her ground.

'But it's important,' he said. 'He'll make time for me.'

'Not now, Mr Latchford. We're about to have a seance. You should leave.'

He looked around and seemed startled to find us there too.

'I only need one minute.'

'I'm sorry. You'll have to make an appointment.'

'I've as much right as anyone else to be here. More, probably. I've paid my dues. And Vivian knows on which side his bread is buttered. We have important matters to discuss.'

'You can see him after the seance, but you'll have to wait.'

He glared at her.

'I'll be back,' he said.

She let him out again, slamming the door behind him. Roz did not seem put out by this contretemps. She took my unwilling arm and steered me inside.

We followed Titania through a beaded curtain into a similarly ill-lit room with a round table covered in a deep red tablecloth. A large crystal ball on a three-legged stand occupied the centre of the table. Oil paintings of random Victorians in costume bedecked the walls, interspersed with candle holder brackets. The smell of patchouli permeated the air, and I could have sworn I caught a whiff of spliff as well.

A tall, strikingly handsome man stood to one side of the table, watching us enter with narrowed eyes. He had black hair and plucked eyebrows, and wrinkle-free moisturised skin. I detected some eyeliner too. A showman. He brought his manicured hands together in a steeple.

'My dear Roz,' he said. 'And you've brought a friend. How nice.'

The honeyed tone of his voice was laced with cyanide. I felt a shiver run up my back. Not a man to be trifled with, whatever I thought of his act.

'My name's Tanya Bowe,' I said.

'I don't need your name, just your obedience,' he hissed. I stifled the urge to laugh. 'Sit in that chair and be absolutely silent. Don't move, don't cough, don't speak.'

I almost asked him if I could breathe, but I didn't want to ruin the moment for Roz who gazed at Blackwood with a fanatic's fervour. I sat meekly in the chair assigned to me and put my hands on my thighs. Roz approached the table and sat facing Blackwood with me beside her. He stared at each member of the group through hooded eyes. Only Raven Huxley held his gaze. I noticed Blackwood smirked to himself.

'How are you all feeling?' he said. 'Did you experience any relief after last week's session?'

'Much better, thank you. I feel lighter somehow,' said Natalee.

He nodded sagely.

'Excellent. We are making significant progress. Your sister is pleased. She is settling in on the other side. It's not easy, you know, crossing over.'

I expected Roz to shoot me a wink at this stage, but she remained passive under his gaze. I couldn't believe it. We had always made fun of people like Vivian in the past - pompous men who thought people hung on their every word. We had spent hours giggling with Ghita over some random blowhard being dethroned on the internet. It felt odd watching Roz kowtow to this serpent without a whisper of protest. I elbowed her, and she yelped. Blackwood shot me a glare.

'Before we assemble the spirits today, I have an announcement to make. I have had a calling from the other side, and I will shortly cross over to the netherworld. It's nothing to worry about. I'll still be with you in spirit. We all transition to the next life eventually.'

'Are you ill?' asked Emily, a trifle eagerly I thought.

'The flesh is weak, but the spirit is strong,' said Blackwood. 'Please don't ask me any more questions.'

A murmur of dissent went up, but Blackwood held up his hand to quiet us. He made us all hold hands. Natalee's hand had the consistency of a wet sponge, but I pretended I didn't notice. Blackwood muttered incantations and called the spirits to join us. I had to stifle a laugh, but he noticed, and a shadow crossed his face. He did not enjoy being doubted.

When the spirits were assembled, Blackwood worked his way around the table, asking people how they were and if they had questions for their relatives. When he got to Roz, she asked him if he had talked to her mother.

'I did. She asked me to tell you she's sorry about your argument. She wanted to make it up to you, but she got called away too soon. Does the name Vinnie mean anything to you?'

Roz gasped and dropped her head into her hands. Her sobs escaped through her fingers.

'Who's Vinnie?' I asked. Blackwood flashed me a warning glance. 'Roz doesn't know anyone called Vinnie.'

His face darkened with fury. Roz tugged at my arm and shook her head.

'I do,' she said. 'It's me.'

'What? How on earth does he know that?'

'My mother told him.'

'You're joking, right?'

'Please stop talking. You'll disturb the spirits,' said Blackwood.

I should have shut up there and then, but I couldn't escape the feeling it was all a giant con.

'What spirits? Something funny is going on here,' I said.

'Your friend seems uncomfortable,' Blackwood said to Roz. 'Maybe she should wait in the vestibule?'

'But I don't want to.'

'We want you to,' said Natalee. 'Please.'

'Will you be okay without me?' I asked Roz.

'I'll be fine,' said Roz. 'I'll be out in a while. Don't worry about me.'

Disappointed to be ejected I pushed my way through the bead curtains and almost bumped into Titania who appeared to be looking at Roz's phone. She held it behind her back when I came out, her face white with guilt.

'Did he throw you out?' she said. 'He doesn't like non-believers in the inner sanctum. It disturbs the communication with the spirit world.'

'Actually, I felt faint.'

'Oh, maybe they tried to use you as a vessel. That can happen you know, but usually you need to believe.'

'And who told you I didn't?'

'Oh, I can tell. Most times, anyway.'

'Maybe you got it wrong this time. Do you have the gift too?'

She turned as pink as a peony and shook her head.

'Of course not. I don't even…'

She trailed off and looked uncomfortable.

'I've got work to do. I need you to wait outside.'

'Outside? But I'd rather wait indoors.'

'You can't stay here. You will interfere with the—'

'Communication from the spirit world. Yes, I get the picture. Can you tell Roz I'll wait in the car? I need my phone.'

She turned, and I glimpsed the phone she held in her hand. Definitely Roz's. Mouse had given us all a strict lecture about password-protecting our phones. I had a new Android phone that used my fingerprint, but it hardly ever worked as my index fingerprint was so shallow the scanner could not read it easily. It didn't matter, as I had refused to put my bank details on my phone and used my debit card instead. I couldn't rid myself of the feeling that someone might empty my pathetic account one day and leave me penniless. Mouse rolled his eyes at me, but I refused to give in. Roz used a password, which she had memorised. She had an almost didactic memory for numbers and could still recite our telephone numbers from the old days of rotary dial phones.

I entered the lift and descended to the ground floor. Outside, the sun had come out and warmed the air to a pleasant temperature. The man Titania had called Mr Latchford was smoking a cigarette in front of the building. My curiosity was piqued by his argument with Titania.

'You're Craig Latchford, aren't you?' I asked.

'What's it to you?' he said, turning his shoulder to me.

'I think my friend Ghita Chowdhury worked with you at the Seacastle Council?'

He stiffened and did not turn around.

'I don't remember such a person.'

'She used to be in procurement, but now she's in planning.'

It was as if the sun had come out from behind a cloud. He did a double take and turned to me.

'Ghita Chowdhury, of course I remember. She's a charming woman, very charming. We should get together sometime and have a drink.'

'She works part time at my shop, Second Home, if you want to drop by for coffee.'

'Does she now? I might just do that.'

He stubbed his cigarette butt out on the pavement and walked towards an expensive-looking car. I resisted the temptation to tell him to pick it up and put it in a dustbin since I couldn't see one in the vicinity. Instead, I collected it with a tissue and wrapped it up. There's never a dustbin when you need one.

While I waited for Roz, I sat on a bench on the promenade and watched the herring gulls soar and bicker over Seacastle. I wondered if my gull friend Herbert flew among them. I had fed him bacon rinds and sandwich crusts since he was a fledging, but always from the wind shelter near the Grotty Hovel. He had never ventured near me anywhere else as far as I knew. Two gulls landed nearby on the sea wall and waddled up and down before chorusing together. I smiled at their cheek when they ignored passers-by who could have reached out and touched them.

Even as I enjoyed the view of the beach and its inhabitants, a creeping feeling of unease came over me as I surveyed the scene. The entire performance involving the phones by the medium's assistant had worried me. Titania did not strike me as trustworthy, but was I judging a book by its cover? Being covered in tattoos and piercings is such a normal look for young people. Had I let my upbringing prejudice my reaction to her? We were brought up to associate tattoos with criminals and sailors. I found it hard to stop my brain from immediately judging someone on their appearance. But then, didn't Titania label me as an interfering old biddy from her first glance? Her assessment may even have held more truth than mine. Perhaps Vivian Blackwood was just trying to make a living using his skills as an empath? Where was the harm in that? He probably had loads of rules about spirits just to make himself seem more mysterious. I laughed out loud as I remembered his exasperation when I didn't play along.

'What are you laughing about all by yourself?' said Roz, coming up behind me. She sat on the bench and passed me a large Mr Whippy ice cream with a flake sticking out of it. We sat in silence, gazing out to sea and licking our ice creams. Roz seemed content after her visit to Vivian Blackwood, and I had no intention of letting my doubts upset her again. She cleared her throat.

'I know you think Vivian's a fake,' she said. 'But he knows things I haven't ever told anyone. If he's a fraud, how come he knows the pet name my mother used to call me?'

'Vinnie?'

'Exactly.'

Chapter 4

I dropped Roz back to the harbour and drove to Second Home to help Mouse in the shop. Roz's conviction that Blackwood had communicated with her mother worried me. It might be beneficial for her to see him if it brought her comfort, but what if she found out he had strung her along? And how did he know the private details of Roz's relationship with her mother?

I parked the car near the shop for once and bought some chocolate croissants for our coffee at the French bakery, which had recently opened. The smell of the pastries made me drool, so I texted Mouse to make us a coffee before I got out of the car. The flaky pastry warmed my hands through the thin paper bag, which was stained with butter leaking from the croissants. The anticipation made me increase my pace, and I arrived at the shop panting.

'Wow, they smell amazing,' said Mouse. 'I'm just frothing the milk.'

We sat together in the window seat and munched our way through a croissant each, making appreciative noises.

'Tell me about the medium,' said Mouse. 'Was she dressed in a kaftan and a turban?'

'Actually, it was a he, not a she. Vivian Blackwood.'

'The Vivian Blackwood? Did you speak to him?'

'Not really. He threw me out when I tried to interfere with the proceedings.'

Mouse rolled his eyes.

'Honestly. You missed your chance to see a master in action. I bet you'd have discovered how he winkles people's secrets out of them.'

'Maybe. According to Roz, he knew things nobody else should know, except for her and her mother.'

'That sounds fishy. Are you sure he didn't get his information from the internet?'

'The internet? I didn't think of that. Why don't you search for Sarah Barrow and Roz Murray and see what you can come up with?'

Mouse removed his tablet from his satchel and soon became absorbed in scouting out information and getting stymied by dead ends. I washed out the cups and cleaned the coffee machine, glancing over to observe him now and then. He had matured into a stunning young man with black curls and soulful grey eyes, and he had a habit of pouting when he concentrated, which must have driven the girls at his university wild. I wasn't sure why he hadn't found a gorgeous partner yet. His intensity might have put the average person of his age off, but any university held a wide selection of eccentrics and intellectuals within its walls. He had embarked on several abortive relationships since moving in with me, but he seemed to prefer hanging out at home with me and Harry and getting cuddles from Hades.

'He's just picky,' said Harry when I commented. 'You should think yourself lucky he doesn't bring a parade of short-term girlfriends, whose names we can't remember, to the Grotty Hovel. They'd only use your makeup and steal your perfume.'

He had a point. And I had suffered from jealousy for a while when Mouse chose someone unsuitable. I found it hard to be a new mother at my age. I needed more time with him before he fled the nest, but I also wanted him to find someone lovely with whom to be happy.

Mouse dropped his tablet onto the table with a theatrical sigh.

'I can't find anything,' he said. 'The death notice is as dry as dust. There are no details about Sarah Barrow or Roz Murray, except for their relationship as mother and daughter. Sarah Barrow doesn't have an online presence at all. It's as if she never existed.'

'I expect that's more common than you imagine for women of her vintage. I doubt she ever used the internet to book a flight or buy something. Roz had to convince her to buy a mobile phone so she could keep an eye on her.'

'She tracked her?'

'The parent-child relationship often switches when people reach an advanced age. It stops people wandering off and getting lost when their memories go.'

'Did you track me when you got your phone?'

'Don't be ridiculous. I could hardly send a text when I met you. I'm still not that internet-savvy.'

'Sarah Barrow certainly wasn't. I can't find her anywhere.'

'What about Roz?'

'Are you sure we should check up on her?'

'We're not prying. We're trying to protect her from Vivian Blackwood. There's something not quite right about that man. Look under her maiden name as well.'

'I forgot about that. Roz Barrow, of course.'

I left him to it while I served a couple who were interested in a Lloyd Loom armchair I had downstairs. The woman did not want to pay what I asked, and the ruder she became the less inclined I felt to reduce the price. Finally, her husband took out his wallet and handed me the full price in cash.

'I don't know why you bother,' he said. 'It's hardly going to break the bank.'

He picked up the chair and walked out of the shop followed by his disgruntled spouse who threw me a look of loathing as she left. I wasn't sure if he had been talking to me or to her, but a sale's a sale. I turned to listen to Mouse speaking from the café above me.

'I can't find anything yet,' said Mouse. 'Leave it with me and I'll have a deep dive later.'

'Be careful. I know your degree is teaching you many methods to get your hands on private information, but we don't have permission for any of this.'

'I promise. Public information only.'

So Blackwood hadn't got his insights from the internet. I racked my brains trying to imagine how else he might have found out about Roz and her relationship with her mother.

'He must have found out somewhere. I simply don't believe he is psychic. There's something funny going on.'

'I should've known you'd be criticising Vivian,' said a voice. 'You can't leave well alone. You always investigate everything.'

Roz had come in through the door left open by the couple and stood behind me, but I hadn't seen her. I spun to face her to apologise, but she didn't let me.

'Oh, you're sorry now. Of course you are. I heard you disrespecting my choices. Well, I like Vivian, and he's doing me good, so you can keep your nose out of my business, and your Mouse too,' she shouted.

She left the shop again, slamming the door. I felt awful. She was right. I couldn't help myself. The reason I had been successful as an investigative journalist was that I suffered from congenital curiosity and I couldn't leave well alone. Mouse came downstairs shamefaced and sighed.

'I feel terrible now,' he said.

'It's not your fault. I'm the one who should have left well alone. Let's agree to let Roz do whatever she needs to in order to recover from her mother's death. I promise not to investigate any further, and you should stop your search too.'

'Definitely. I hate to see her so upset. We were only trying to help.'

'She knows that. She'll forgive us. Don't do anymore searching for now. I'll speak to her later and apologise.'

Luckily, we had a good number of clients during the rest of the afternoon and had no more time to dwell on

Roz. The people who come into Second Home are either young trendsetters who thought I sold antiques and want to fill their house with retro goods, or older people with a bout of nostalgia or light wallets. Even though they could buy wonderful stuff cheap at Second Home, people with 'new' money preferred to pay triple for the same items from the Asian Antique Emporium run by Max and Grace Wong, my upmarket rivals further down the High Street. I tucked the day's takings into my handbag.

We shut the shop and drove to the supermarket to buy groceries to stock up the kitchen, and a rack of lamb to celebrate, courtesy of the Lloyd Loom. It was also Harry's favourite meat. Harry loved traditional British fare. His years in the army eating out of tins or canteens had made him a massive fan. We also bought new potatoes and broccoli and a head of spring greens. I should have been looking forward to supper, but I couldn't rid myself of the shame I felt for hurting Roz. Sometimes I didn't know when to stop.

Chapter 5

I couldn't sleep a wink all night because my brain wouldn't shut down. Harry had an important meeting the next day, so I forced myself to leave him in the land of Nod, oblivious to my self-imposed distress. I lay beside him, wide-eyed and fretting, reworking scenarios where I had behaved better and Roz didn't get upset with me. No matter how much I berated myself, I still couldn't rid myself of the conviction Vivian Blackwood was a complete charlatan with no good intentions behind his sophistry. I had zero proof, but my intuition yelled at me and kept my shame company. They played happily together and kept me up for hours.

The next morning, after Harry had left, I dragged myself out of bed and took a long shower. As the hot water coursed down my back, I examined my options for dealing with Roz. I knew we would sort it out. We always had in the past. But I had underestimated the strength of her attachment to Blackwood and his apparent ability to contact her deceased mother. Would I talk to my mother again if I could? Or would I leave well enough alone? I might be keener to speak to my father, with whom I had much more in common. But they had been dead for years and I couldn't magic them up again, no matter how much I wanted to.

The solution to my problem lived in a house two streets away - my older sister Helen. We had become much closer after she moved to Seacastle, and closer still since she had taken George off my hands. He had already divorced me by then and had an unsuccessful relationship with my replacement. Once I saw George and Helen together, it became blindingly obvious he had married the wrong sister from the start. When people asked me if I minded, I told them we were all happier now, so not at all. Despite my irritation at some of her habits and her old-lady ideas, I respected her and her sound, sisterly advice. I got dressed and put my hair up in a bun before ringing her and asking if I could come over for a cup of tea. I could tell from her voice she knew what ailed me, but she did not question me on the telephone. I put on my coat and grabbed a packet of Hobnobs to take to her as a peace offering.

Helen came to the door and gave me a warm hug. I sank into her sisterly arms and cried. I hadn't meant to, but my restless night had left me vulnerable, and there's no safer place than an elder sibling's hug. Who understands you better? Unfortunately, this means they have also earned the right to criticise you with well-aimed barbs.

'Roz rang me,' she said. 'Honestly, what are you like?'

'But—'

'Don't but me. Come in. The kettle's on.'

'Actually, there is no but. I didn't like her seeing a medium, and I should have kept it to myself.'

'He's actually pretty good. I don't know why you've jumped to conclusions.'

I couldn't believe what I was hearing. Helen, the Uber-sceptic, knew Vivian Blackwood?

'You're kidding, right?'

'Not in the slightest.'

'Am I to understand that you've been to see him too?'

She turned away to fill the teapot with boiling water. The tips of her ears turned pink. I could almost feel the heat.

'You have. What possessed you?'

'No wonder Roz is cross with you. I'm a grown-up. I'm allowed to seek comfort with a professional.'

'A professional?' I spluttered. 'A professional what? That's the question. Why on earth did you go to see him?'

She turned to me with a pleading expression on her face.

'I miss our mother. Sarah's funeral made me realise just how much. I couldn't get Mum out of my head. I would pay a million pounds for one more hour with her. You wouldn't understand.'

She was right. I didn't, but I had no intention of admitting it.

'I miss them too, you know. Just not enough for reincarnation to be an option.'

'Vivian doesn't claim to reincarnate anyone.'

'Vivian? You're on a first-name basis with this charlatan? What does George say?'

Her face froze. She stirred the teapot to play for time and poured us both a cup of tea. I sat at the kitchen table waiting for her to explain. She bit her lip.

'Okay, you've got me. George doesn't know. He'd never understand even if I tried to explain. And he'd have a fit if he knew how much it cost.'

I could only imagine. George had always been a little tight with money. Vivian's fee might give him some sort of fit.

'A conniption,' I said. 'Definitely one of those.'

We both laughed.

'Where is he today?'

'Oh, he's got a murder at a block of flats on the beach road. No doubt he'll be late home tonight as usual.'

'I don't envy you. I don't miss being married to a detective. What should I do about Roz? You're so much better at compromise than I am.'

'Look. As I told Roz, you are a nonbeliever. You're a Doubting Thomas. You want to touch the wounds before you will accept they exist.'

'It's not like that at all. I'm suspicious because he knows things he shouldn't. I'm trying to protect her until I know how he got hold of the information.'

'But what if he's the genuine article? What if he can really talk to the dead? There have been cases of genuine mediums, you know.'

I had never heard of one, but I didn't want to say so.

'I'm not saying it's impossible. I'm just worried that he belongs to the ninety-nine per cent of mediums who operate by reading people's unhappiness, or their internet profiles.'

'Fair enough. Can't you do your research without upsetting Roz?'

'I guess so. Mouse is on the job. I told him to stop, but there's no chance of that. He's like a dog with a bone.'

We finished our tea. Helen told me all about her daughter Olivia's gap-year adventures in Australia, and I made admiring noises in the right places. In truth, Olivia seemed to have matured considerably since she had stayed at Shelley Road when Gladys's house was an Airbnb. Mouse had had a crush on her then. I didn't know whether he still harboured feelings. Since they were not blood relations, I didn't see any harm in it. I glanced at my watch.

'I've got to go,' I said. 'Mouse is alone in the shop, and it can get busy at coffee time.'

'It's always coffee time at Second Home.'

'True. You should pop in and see us there. Maybe you'd find something nice for your house.'

She blushed and wouldn't look at me.

'What?'

'I'm trying not to buy anything else until I move,' she said.

'You're moving? Again. But… Oh.'

'George thinks it's silly for us to run two households. He wants me to live with him.'

'In the beige palace? But that's wonderful news. Why didn't you tell me?'

'I didn't know how you'd take it. You were married to him once.'

'Yeah, but not now. I think it's fantastic. I'm happy for you both.'

She smiled shyly.

'Me too,' she said.

I ambled along the promenade, enjoying the balmy weather and trying to organise my thoughts. Helen and George living in the same house? Now that I thought about it, it was a little weird, but not before time. George had fallen head over heels with my older sister, and I couldn't begrudge them their happiness. As long as they didn't want Mouse. I would fight to the death to keep him with me. I turned onto King Street and then onto the High Street. Mouse had put some rather nice kitchen chairs with red vinyl backrests in the window set back from a table with a yellow Formica top. It looked quite chic for once.

Inspired by Mouse's creativity, I set to work reinvigorating the décor in the café. We had always used stock to furnish it, and I didn't intend to reinvent the wheel, but I wanted to make it more welcoming and less random. We spent hours bringing furniture upstairs and taking it back down after it didn't match the way we had imagined. We had to stop for lunch when all the young folk from the offices came in to eat their sandwiches with a beverage. I didn't mind them bringing their own lunch. I did not have the facilities to provide anything other than coffee and cake, and they often returned on weekends to buy both. After rush hour at the Vintage, Mouse helped me do the accounts for the month and pay some pending bills. We had had quite a profitable month, so I decided to find some nice matching crockery for the Vintage. We had started the café with mismatched cups and saucers from the charity shops, which monopolised our end of the High Street, but the time had come to upgrade.

Mouse and I spent a pleasant hour choosing several sets of rather snazzy, brightly coloured, modern crockery from an outlet on the net. After we had ordered it, he caught my eye, and I guessed what he was about to say.

'I did some more research,' he said. 'I know you told me not to, but I couldn't help it.'

Before I had a chance to scold him, my mobile phone rang. Helen. Had I forgotten something at her house?

'Hi Sis. What's up?'

'I've had the most terrible news. It's George.'

'George? Has something happened to him?'

Mouse looked up from his tablet and stared at me.

'No, not to him. Remember I told you he attended a murder scene this morning?'

I shook my head at Mouse and rolled my eyes. His face relaxed.

'Yes. What about it? Do we know the victim?'

'We were talking about him. Vivian Blackwood has been found dead in his flat.'

'What? That's awful. Are you sure he was murdered?'

'George told me somebody bludgeoned him to death. I can't believe it. Who would do such a thing?'

'I have no idea. Perhaps a poltergeist?'

'Honestly, you have no respect for people's feelings. No wonder Roz is furious with you.'

'I'm sorry. You know I use humour to diffuse tense situations. It's like a nervous tic.'

'You're no good at it.'

She hung up.

'Who's dead?' asked Mouse.

'Vivian Blackwood.'

'Now that's genuinely spooky. Didn't he tell you he would cross over soon? Wait until you hear what I found on the internet.'

'Tell your father. It's his investigation.'

'Really? Don't you want to know?'

'I do, but I promised Roz I wouldn't investigate Blackwood while he was alive. And I'm going to let George investigate him now that he's dead.'

Chapter 6

I meant to keep my promise to Helen and Roz, but my resolution was soon tested. Before that, I had to sort out a van full of furniture from Harry's cousin Tommy in London. Usually, Harry took goods I couldn't sell at Second Home up to Tommy's warehouse in the East End in our van. He sold them or scrapped them depending on whether they could be upcycled or not. This time, Tommy had done a clearance for one of their extended family's elderly cousins, and Harry had chosen some pieces he thought we could sell. I waited with trepidation for him to arrive in the van. Unlike Mouse, Harry had never got the hang of the vintage market. He simply couldn't tell whether anything was saleable. I had given up bringing him to boot sales, as he could not be trusted with Second Home's hard-earned cash. He had loads of enthusiasm, but zero taste.

Harry arrived in a great mood, and we emptied the van.

'Where's the mouse?' said Harry. 'I bet he ran away when he heard I was arriving.'

'No, he didn't. He's at the dentist. He'll help when he gets back.'

To my delight, Harry had come up trumps by sticking to the rules I had given him about choosing plain, light-hued wood and vinyl-covered furniture, or bright lamps and vases from Habitat or Heals. By coincidence, he brought me a set of four sky-blue versions of the chairs in my shop window, and they looked stunning when placed among the others.

'Did I do well?' he asked me.

'You are a genius,' I said, giving him a kiss on top of his bald dome.

Some of the other pieces were not as successful, but I didn't say so. I put them in the back room, ready for mixing with the next load we sent up to London. Harry would never notice, and if someone wanted to buy them, all the better. Harry had inherited the business from an uncle, and we had met when I moved into the Grotty Hovel, and he was clearing the house next door. He found Hades in a laundry basket, and the rest is history. Everything that happens has a positive side, and I always try to remember it when my plans fail.

'My ghast is flabbered,' he said, when I told him about Vivian Blackwood. 'Roz and Helen? I wonder who else we know were clients of his.'

'One client who didn't like what he heard there.'

'Not necessarily. Doesn't George look at love interests first?'

'Maybe they were both a lover and a client?'

'Like you and me?'

I punched his arm, and he laughed.

'Let's have a coffee. I've been daydreaming about Ghita's cakes all the way from London.'

We hadn't been upstairs long when George turned up pale and shaken. Harry made him eat a piece of coffee walnut cake while I prepared a cappuccino for him. He hardly seemed to notice his cake, which was unusual. Coffee walnut was one of his absolute favourites of Ghita's cakes, and he liked to make appreciative noises as he devoured it. I exchanged glances with Harry.

'All right, mate? You look a little peaky?'

'Oh, I'm perfectly healthy, just rather shocked. Did Tanya tell you about the murder of the local medium?'

'Yes, I think she mentioned it.'

Only one hundred times.

'What I'm going to tell you is confidential, but I can't talk about it at the station.'

'You mean about Helen seeing him?' I asked. 'She already told me. That's going to make it a little complicated. Is she a suspect?'

George's jaw dropped almost onto the floor, and I realised I had made a massive blunder. I resisted the urge to put my head in my hands. Harry faked a cough, but I refused to look at him. I risked a glance at George. His jaw worked as he struggled to contain himself. Oops.

'She's done what?' he said. 'This is the final straw. It's bad enough DI Antrim is involved, but now Helen. I may have to step aside from this case.'

My ears pricked up.

'Did you say DI Antrim? How is Terry involved?'

Harry sneered at the mention of DI Antrim, but he said nothing.

'The silly fool was the last person to see Blackwood alive.'

'But what was he doing there? Was it connected to an investigation?'

George sighed.

'He had an appointment.'

I almost laughed at his crestfallen expression.

'With the medium? I don't Adam and Eve it,' said Harry.

'And what was Helen doing there?' said George. 'You need to tell me everything.'

'You'll have to ask her,' I said. 'Is there any way you can pretend you saw her name in the appointment book? She made me swear I wouldn't tell you about her seeing him. Only when you said it was confidential, I presumed.'

'Honestly. What does it matter how I found out?'

'Please, George.'

'Okay. But it doesn't change the fact that Helen, Terry and half the town are suspects.'

'And Roz,' I said. 'And me, but I didn't have an appointment.'

I thought George would burst a blood vessel.

'Why were you there?'

I decided the truth might be better than inventing some ludicrous excuse, which would only annoy him.

'I went with Roz because I was worried about her seeing a medium.'

George blinked and waited.

'He was running some sort of racket. Well, I don't have any proof of that, but he knew too much about Roz and her mother. It wasn't information that was publicly available.'

'And you know this how? Ah, wait, don't tell me. My son has been doing a bit of snooping on the internet.'

'We stopped. Honestly. We only checked if Roz's mother had left private information on the internet that he could use.'

'And did she?'

'No. I don't think she ever used a computer. Roz forced her to have a mobile phone so she could…'

'So she could do what?'

'Um, track her.'

'Track her?'

'Sarah Barrow had mild dementia. Roz used to track her to make sure she didn't wander off and get lost.'

'I'll pretend you didn't tell me that,' said George. 'Did you confront Blackwood in any way?'

'No, he asked me to leave because I tried to intervene in the seance, so I did.'

'That's all?'

'That's all.'

'Did you see him talking to anyone else?'

'Not apart from the members of the seance. A man turned up to speak to Blackwood, but his assistant, Titania Grafton, sent him away. She has ears like a bat. I bet she knows all about his clients. The good, the bad and the ethereal.'

'I think she's the one who discovered the body. She claims to have heard an altercation as she was leaving the office.'

'When did DI Antrim have his appointment?' said Harry.

'About the time she heard the altercation,' said George. 'It isn't looking good to be honest.'

'How can you say that?' I said with indignation rising in my chest. 'You're not seriously suggesting Terry murdered Vivian Blackwood?'

George picked at the crumbs on his plate.

'I can't believe he'd do a thing like that. He's as straight as an arrow. But I have to follow the evidence. Right now, I have a witness who places DI Antrim at the scene of the crime about the same time as the victim was murdered. There's nothing definitive in that. Flo is at the scene now, collecting the forensic evidence with the rest of the team. The SOCOs will report back to me when they have finished.'

'How do you know Titania is telling the truth?' I asked.

'I don't. But I haven't questioned DI Antrim yet, so he's the nearest we have to a witness so far.'

'When did Blackwood die?' said Harry.

'Sometime yesterday afternoon or early evening. We're not sure yet. Again, Flo will give us an estimate after she finishes up at the scene.'

'Well, that's a turn up for the books,' said Harry. 'I knew DI Antrim was a dodgy geezer right from the start.'

'Don't be ridiculous,' I said. 'You're just jealous because we're friends.'

'He's not your friend,' said George. 'He's mine. Who takes him out for a pint in Brighton?'

'That's business,' I said.

'And your friendship is a pleasure?' said Harry.

'It's professional,' I said. 'We're colleagues.'

'If you ask me, it sounds like a kindergarten up here,' said Mouse, coming up the stairs. 'He's my friend. No, he's mine. I can't believe what I'm hearing.'

'Less of the cheek,' said George. 'Do you have any information on Vivian Blackwood? I understand you've been carrying out some extracurricular searches on the internet.'

Mouse's face showed his reaction to this query.

'Have another piece of cake,' I said. 'You'll need it.'

Chapter 7

George's revelation about Terry Antrim being the last person to see Vivian Blackwood alive gave us all food for thought. Harry, Mouse and I discussed this titbit at home during our supper.

'Maybe some ectoplasm has contaminated the Seacastle water supply like in Ghostbusters 2 and made everyone want to speak to spirits,' said Mouse.

'Nobody watched that film,' I said.

'That's not true. I did,' he said.

I raised an eyebrow, and he dropped the suggestion.

'We're dealing with reality. Why would Terry Antrim bludgeon a medium to death? I doubt he has the strength for a start,' I said.

'A piece of string has more muscles,' said Harry. 'Did I tell you the one about the piece of string who goes into a bar?'

We both groaned.

'Hundreds of times,' said Mouse.

'I'm a frayed knot,' I said.

Harry pouted.

'It's a good joke. One of the best.'

'I wouldn't exaggerate,' I said. 'Anyway, we were talking about Terry Antrim.'

'Him,' said Harry. 'Your other boyfriend.'

'He's her work boyfriend,' said Mouse. 'Does she complain when you cuddle Ghita and Roz in the shop?'

I tried not to laugh. Harry looked miffed.

'No, but that's completely different. That man has a crush on my girlfriend. I don't like it.'

'But Ghita has a ginormous crush on you, or haven't you noticed?' I said.

Harry looked around for backup and, seeing none, grabbed Hades for a snuggle instead.

'Why would Terry see a medium?' asked Mouse.

'I can't imagine. Maybe…'

I trailed off. I know exactly why.

'What?' said Harry, lifting his head out of Hades's fur.

'Terry's son Duncan died of an overdose several years ago. Maybe he wanted to contact him.'

Harry sat up and stared at me.

'You never told me that.'

'Didn't I? Well it was a while ago on the coven murder case. Actually, I had been worried about Mouse staying out late all the time, and I can't remember why I told Terry. But anyway, he told me about losing his son. That's why he's so sad all the time. He's never got over it. So he hasn't got a crush on me.'

'You didn't tell me you were worried about me,' said Mouse.

'I didn't know where I stood with you in the beginning. I was afraid you'd leave if I kept questioning you.'

'Like Dad?'

'Exactly. Anyway, Terry thinks I'm someone he can tell things to without everyone in town knowing about them.'

'That's probably why he didn't tell Roz,' said Mouse, making us all laugh.

'He must have been desperate to go to a medium,' said Harry. 'Doesn't he have a wife he can talk to?'

'She won't talk to him about their son. Antrim told me she locked her memories of Duncan in some inaccessible part of her brain and carries on like he never existed.'

'You sure know how to make a bloke feel guilty,' said Harry.

'I'm sorry. I didn't mean to. He told me in confidence, and I had almost forgotten.'

'You're weird,' said Mouse.

'Better than blabbing,' said Harry. 'I promise to behave better next time I meet him.'

The doorbell rang as he finished his sentence. Mouse opened it and stepped back, his eyes wide.

'Um, it's DI Antrim,' he said.

Terry Antrim hesitated outside the doorway, almost invisible in his dark clothes. He resembled the Grim Reaper in his black hooded windcheater. All he was missing was a scythe. The hollows of his face were in shadow under his prominent brow and hooded eyebrows.

'Have I come at a bad time?' he said.

Harry muttered under his breath.

'Speak of the devil and he will appear.'

I dug my elbow into his ribs and jumped up.

'Why don't you come in? We've just finished supper. I'm sure you're hungry, and there's plenty left. May I serve you a plate?'

'Oh, no, yes, please. Well, if you're sure. I haven't eaten since breakfast.'

'You'll need a beer to wash that down with,' said Harry, scurrying to the fridge.

Soon, Terry sat at the table, making his way through a plate of roast chicken and vegetables. He ate with precise movements, surgically removing the meat from the bone and chewing rhythmically. He sighed with pleasure as he mopped up the gravy with a piece of baked potato.

'That was so delicious. Thank you, Miz Bowe.'

'Oh, Mouse cooked it,' I said, smiling at his use of my surname. He had always called me Miz Bowe as a sort of old-fashioned joke.

'He did? Splendid. A credit to his parents.'

Mouse coloured and looked embarrassed.

'To what do we owe the pleasure of your visit?' I said, although it was pretty obvious to everyone.

'I wondered if I might have a word, in private,' he said. 'If that's all right?'

'I'd rather stay,' said Harry.

'Me too,' said Mouse.

'Look,' I said. 'I'm going to tell them anyway, so you might as well make yourself comfortable in the armchair and tell us all about it.'

Terry sighed and sat down on the couch. Harry refilled his glass. It hadn't escaped my notice that Hades made a beeline for Terry the minute he arranged his gangly limbs on the couch. I watched fascinated as Hades purred like a well-tuned Maserati engine in response to Terry's spindly fingers scratching his ears and chin. Hades was fussy. If he didn't like someone, I took notice. George despaired of me using my cat as a judge of character, but Hades hadn't been wrong yet.

'It's about Vivian Blackwood's murder,' said Terry. 'I'm sure George told you I attended Blackwood's last appointment of the day. I couldn't believe it when I heard someone had bludgeoned him to death after I left.'

'The thing I found strange,' I said, 'is finding out you were visiting a medium. I wouldn't have thought you believed in that sort of thing.'

'Fair enough. I can't really explain it myself.'

'But then I discovered that my sister Helen and my friend Roz also went to see him, so he must have been a great comfort to you all,' I said.

'Well, you know about my son, Duncan, so it won't surprise you he was the reason I went. My wife will not talk about him. She's um, well, she doesn't, she can't...'

Terry flapped his hands in the air like flightless rooks. He seemed unable to articulate for a while. We sat in silence willing him to speak again.

'Um, anyway, I found talking about Duncan to be most therapeutic. Blackwood is only interested in money, but boy can he spin a yarn. He almost had me convinced he could communicate with Duncan. It did me a lot of good. But the last time I saw him; he started asking for money. He knew things about my police cases he shouldn't have known. I think he meant to blackmail me. I lost my temper and grabbed him by the collar. But that's all. I let go again and stormed out of his office. I couldn't believe I'd been stupid enough to confide in him. What worries me is where on earth he got the information from. I could get fired if anyone knew about it.'

He faltered and drank his beer. I wondered if he knew he had just given us an obvious motive for murder. His entire career could have been ruined if Blackwood had carried out his threats.

'That must have been unsettling,' I said. 'How could he have had access to that information?'

Terry shook his head.

'I don't know. I wonder if he hypnotised me? Maybe he extracted the information from me while I was in a trance. I know I often felt dizzy after our sessions, but I presumed it was the flood of emotions disorienting me. I'm not used to strong feelings. I keep everything bottled up.'

'Me too,' muttered Harry.

'Anyway, when I heard about the murder, I knew I'd be a prime suspect for it. I'm sure I left DNA on his clothing when I grabbed him. And I was the last person to see him.'

'Except the murderer,' said Mouse.

'Of course,' I said.

Terry put his head in his hands; his straight black hair interlaced with his thin fingers.

'I didn't do it,' he said. 'I swear. You believe me don't you?'

'Yes,' I said.

'Look, we've not always seen eye to eye, but I think we're friends, and I really don't have any others. I want you to investigate the case and find out who killed Vivian Blackwood.'

'I'm not sure I can do that,' I said.

'They're probably going to arrest me and put me in a cell. I won't be able to prove my innocence from there. Please Tanya. You're the best investigator I know, bar none. If anyone can find out what happened, it's you.'

'He's right, Mum. You're the best. I'll help. I already found out stuff I haven't told you.'

'What do you think, Harry?'

'You know what I think.'

'Okay,' I said. 'I'll do it, but whatever I find out goes straight to George. Good or bad. I won't hide anything from the police investigation.'

'It's a deal. I know I didn't kill him. It's up to you to prove it to everyone else.'

'I'll drink to that,' said Harry.

Chapter 8

Harry and I sat up late into the night discussing Terry Antrim and his odd request. We argued back and forth, but couldn't come up with any reason he would want me to investigate.

'If he's so innocent, how come he won't let George deal with it?' said Harry.

'I don't know. But something's not right and I can't put my finger on it.'

'Why don't you put your finger here? Lower. Lower.'

Honestly. It's hard to focus on a case when you're going out with one.

Early the next morning, I found Mouse sitting on the sofa wrapped in a duvet. He was typing something into his tablet and then scrolling down pages on the internet with the concentration of a born hacker.

'What are you up to?' I asked. 'I hope you've been to bed at least.'

He looked up at me and gave me a sleepy grin.

'Not for long. I've been researching Vivian Blackwood. There are dozens of testimonials on his website all saying similar things.'

'Like what?'

'Claiming he prophesied his own death and was a true psychic. And how they started out as sceptics, but he revealed private matters from his communication with their departed relatives, which convinced them he really could speak with the dead. Things only certain people knew but would never tell anyone. Generally because they were deceased.'

'But how could he have discovered this information if it's not on Facebook or Instagram? Could he have used hypnotism without them knowing?' I asked.

'That's possible. He claims to have been trained by Zelda Romano, a pupil of Doris Stokes, the famous medium.'

'Is she still alive?'

'She's living with her daughter in Brighton. Um, when are you going to make up with Roz?'

'Roz? Why do you ask?'

'I've been thinking. She must be lonely. She needs you and Ghita now. Do you want me to do something?'

'What sort of something?'

'She must be shocked about Blackwood's murder. Why don't I tell her you need her help with the investigation? She knew many of his clients, and some of their secrets. She could help you, and it might help her get over her grief if she were busy.'

I felt a wave of shame as I realised what a rotten friend I had been. Since when did 'I told you so', triumph over friendship?

'That's a brilliant idea. Go down to Pirate's Harbour and find her after breakfast. Tell her I'm sorry and we miss her, too.'

'Okay. I will. I saw Ed's boat come in this morning.'

'I thought you told me you got some sleep.'

'I didn't tell you how much.'

'Please take a nap this afternoon. We can shut the shop if we don't have enough people.'

'Rohan might mind it for us.'

'And pigs might fly. He'd charge triple. I'd lose all my clients. Have a shower and I'll make us some bacon sandwiches.'

After Mouse had left for the harbour, I went to sit in the wind shelter on the promenade. I took some bacon rinds and a few crusts of bread with me in a paper bag for Herbert, the herring gull. In truth, I didn't hold out much hope of him turning up, as I had hardly seen him over the spring. I suspected he had chicks to feed and had no time to chat with me about policing in Seacastle, but to my delight a large shape appeared above the shelter and Herbert flopped to the ground in front of me. He greeted me with loud cries and gobbled the food I had brought him with pleasure. Then, without ceremony, he strutted away and lifted into the air, doing a circuit around the shelter before flying away.

I took out my notebook and read my scribblings from the night before. The breeze whipped the pages as I tried to focus on the facts. Then, I retrieved my pen from my handbag and wrote down what Mouse had told me earlier. Zelda Romano could be a rich vein of information about Blackwood's past. He mentioned her on his website only in passing, but several newspaper articles had made more of his reputation and how it linked to her training. I promised myself to leave the cynicism at home when I visited her.

The wind had picked up since I had sat down, and my hair blew around wildly. Seacastle's prevailing wind resembled Ireland's rain in that it was always blowing, about to blow or just finished blowing. I collected my hair in a bunch and forced it into a bun, securing it with a scrunchie. When I looked up from my task, I saw Roz standing in front of me. I leapt to my feet and hugged her hard, whispering how sorry I was in her ear. Her cheeks were wet with tears, which mingled with mine.

'I'm so sorry,' I said.

'No, I'm sorry. Mouse explained to me who Vivian Blackwood really was. I feel I owe it to my mother to find out who killed him and why. It's got to be related to the way Blackwood extracted information from people. He might have done it to me too. Maybe George should check?'

'As far as I know, they are tracing all the payments made to Blackwood over the last five years. We'll soon know how bad it was. Hopefully, it was too soon to cheat you out of any money.'

'So what's your next move?'

'Blackwood learned his trade from a Romany medium called Zelda Romano. I'm hoping we can visit her and discover some of his secrets.'

'Why don't we call Miles Quirk?'

'Miles? Whatever for?'

'He's a witch, remember? He's familiar with everyone in the spiritual community in Brighton. I bet he knows Zelda.'

'I'd completely forgotten. He knows the entire population of Sussex. I'll give Miles a call and see if he can arrange a visit. Do you want to come?'

'Is the Pope a Catholic? Of course I do.'

'Excellent. Let's go to Second Home and have a coffee. We can plan our line of attack at the Vintage.'

'Did I see you talking to a seagull just now?'

'Maybe.'

'And you think I'm nuts?'

We walked along the promenade arm-in-arm and admired the turbines in the distance, which looked like a field of children's windmills turning in the breeze. White-topped waves broke on the pebble banks where a man in an ancient, holey cardigan used a metal detector to search for treasure.

'I found a golf medal on the beach once,' said Roz. 'I never figured out how it got there.'

We turned up King's Street and headed for the shop. Once out of the wind, I gave Miles a call.

'Hi there. Are you busy?'

'I'm always busy, darling.'

'So you're not interested in helping us contact Zelda Romano then?'

'Zelda? Why on earth would you want to… Oh, this is about Vivian Blackwood isn't it?'

'What if it is?'

'I want in.'

'I'll tell you what. You get us an appointment, and you can drive us to Brighton to see her.'

'Great. Wait. What?'

'Come on. You know you want to.'

Chapter 9

Miles picked us up after lunch in his ancient Volvo estate. He looked me up and down and shook his head.

'Honestly, dear. The nineteen-seventies have been over for decades.'

'I'm paying homage,' I said. 'It's a fashion revival. Flares are back.'

He winced.

'Not for long.'

I ignored his comments as he was rude to everyone. He hadn't singled me out. He sashayed over to the car in his exaggerated manner and held the door open.

'Age before beauty,' he said, as Roz got in.

She gave him a frosty glare, which he ignored. She occupied the passenger seat while I sat in the back. The boot contained stacks of ragged cardboard boxes stuffed with random pieces of bubble wrap and old newspapers. I had the feeling Miles never turned down the chance of a bargain. It paid to be prepared. Miles drove as if he had a fragile vase in the car. No wonder he needed an hour to get to Brighton. A pervasive smell of aftershave filled the interior of the car and made me feel slightly nauseous.

'I've been doing some research on mediums,' said Miles.

'Really? What have you come up with?' I asked.

'Have you ever heard of M Lamar Keene?'

'Wasn't he from America?' said Roz.

'That's right. He set himself up as a medium in Tampa in the sixties and seventies. People came from miles around to attend his spiritualist church.'

'Why is he relevant?' I said.

'He wrote a book called The Psychic Mafia, which caused a massive upheaval when it was published in nineteen-seventy-six. Somebody tried to assassinate him after he revealed many mediums shared client information so they could monetise their clients' grief.'

'That sounds familiar.'

'Tell me about it,' said Roz. 'But who shared information with Blackwood about my mother? She turned into a hermit in her last years. She talked to me only when she had to. The health service wanted to give her a carer, but she wouldn't have a stranger in the house.'

'Did he try to extract money from you?' I asked.

'No, but I've a feeling it was only a matter of time.'

'I wonder how many people were being swindled by this awful man,' said Miles.

'George gave me a list of the people at the seance held before his murder.'

'You don't suppose they ganged together like in Murder on the Orient Express?' said Miles. 'You could be Peter Ustinov.'

'They had left before DI Antrim came over,' I said. 'Although it's possible someone hid in a cupboard or something.'

'But how would they do that without Titania knowing about it?' said Roz.

'I'd forgotten about her. What if she knew they were hiding?' I said.

'The plot thickens,' said Miles.

I took out my notebook and wrote Titania's name as a reminder to myself to contact her. Then I leant back and enjoyed the view as we made our way along the coast road to Brighton. The tide had gone out, revealing the mud flats at Shoreham, and dozens of waders were foraging for worms with their long, curved beaks. Small sailing boats lay toppled to one side, stranded like coloured fish on the banks of the shore. Roz's mop of yellow curls bounced in front of the headrest as she tried to get more details about M Lamar Keene out of Miles.

The mid-afternoon traffic was light and fast flowing, but with Miles staying well below the speed limit, we arrived with only ten minutes to spare. It took us that long to find a parking space anywhere near the block where Zelda Romano lived with her daughter. They occupied a converted flat in an Edwardian terraced house on Brighton beach overlooking the remains of the West Pier, which had burned down a decade before. We assembled in the lift and rose to the top floor where Diana Romano held the door open for us.

'I wasn't expecting a delegation,' she said, pursing her lips. 'My mother is poorly and not used to visitors.'

Miles appeared not to hear her, and after pecking her on both cheeks, said, 'Where's the invalid then?'

I heard cackling in the next room, followed by the hacking cough of a lifelong smoker. Miles pushed open the door, releasing a fug of cigarette smoke and whisky fumes. It was like entering a pub in the days before smoking was banned indoors. I had a strong feeling of déjà vu when I spotted the disco ball hanging from the ceiling, covered in reflective mirror chips. The light refracted all around the room as the ball spun on its rope, picking out odd knick-knacks and crystals and reminding me of Perpetua Hastings' Practical Magic shop. In the corner near the window, a bundle of colourful silk skirts and shawls extended a claw, which beckoned us closer. Zelda's face, as wrinkled as a raisin, poked out from behind the wing of the armchair.

'Miles, you young reprobate. Don't you have any time for your old friends anymore?' she said.

Miles hurried to her side, grasping her claw and practically genuflecting.

'Duchess,' he said. 'Looking better than ever, I must say.'

'Don't soft-soap me, dearie. I'm a medium. I can see right through you. And who are these fascinating young women? I believe I've met you before,' she said, pointing at Roz. 'A long time ago though.'

'I don't think so, I—'

'Oh, yes, I remember. You used to hang around with the Brighton Coven, but you don't have a history, do you?'

'She's Roz Murray, and I'm Tanya Bowe,' I said, hoping to distract her.

'Divorced him, did you? So unsuited. I could never understand it myself.'

'How do you…?'

I saw Miles's expression. Competition for Roz. He loved to gossip and relate scandal to anyone who would listen. I suspected he proved a useful conduit for the medium to learn about things she could pretend to sense. I caught her staring at me.

'Your father loved you very much,' she said.

A warm glow hit my heart followed by fury at my reaction to her obvious ploy. Before I could think of a retort, Miles had picked up the whisky and poured a good couple of fingers into her glass.

'Leave Tanya alone. That's not why we're here,' he said.

Zelda sighed and rolled her eyes.

'As if I didn't know. You're wanting to know about Vivian, aren't you? That snake in the grass.'

'You heard what happened to him,' I said.

'I know he's dead. I saw it on the news. What happened?'

I made a quick decision to keep the way he died to myself.

'Somebody murdered him in his office, shortly after he announced he would soon cross over to the netherworld.'

'That's hardly news, dear. The only surprise is how long it took for someone to take him out. The despicable toe-rag.'

'Has he been to see you?' said Miles.

'He wouldn't dare. He's not that stupid.'

Roz flashed me a look. Did she mean after he died, or before? Both, I guessed.

'I understand you were his mentor,' I said. 'You must have known him better than anyone.'

'Better than his mother, I'd say. Not that she wanted anything to do with him.'

'Did he have genuine clairvoyant abilities?' asked Roz.

Zelda laughed, and it caught in her throat, turning into a lung-busting coughing fit. Her daughter tutted.

'She's not well. You shouldn't be disturbing her like this.'

'Oh, shut up, Diana. I almost never have visitors. Leave us alone for a moment, can't you?'

Diana drew her eyebrows together.

'Don't blame me when you drop dead,' she said, and slammed the door on her way out of the room.

'Don't worry about her,' said Zelda. 'Top me up. There's a good chap. Where was I? Oh yes. Vivian didn't have any communication with the spirit world. He was what we call an open eye. He didn't need spirits. He had eyes, ears, and a fast internet connection. Could read a Facebook profile like a palm. Not that he lacked talent.'

She took a sip of her whisky and waved the glass in the air, catching the reflections from the disco ball.

'So he wasn't a complete fraud?' I asked.

'He could read people like books. Every gesture, emotion, tic. He was a genius. But he worked on the dark side.'

'But could he… influence people?' said Roz.

Zelda gave a throaty chuckle.

'He could read a person's wants like a menu. Once you told him your name, he could have you spilling your darkest secrets before you knew it.'

Miles leant forward. 'Did he hypnotise people?'

She shook her head.

'I tried to teach him how to, but he couldn't get the hang of it. I'm not sure why. Anyway, he didn't need to. He could con anyone wide awake.'

'Did you teach him that?' I asked.

Zelda sniffed. 'I taught him how to listen. He taught himself how to manipulate and con people.'

'Do you know anyone who might have wanted to kill him?'

'Most people who ever met him, dearie. Vivian Blackwood was a scumbag of the lowest order. Whoever killed him did the world a favour.'

Chapter 10

Diana Romano soon ran out of patience with our disturbing her mother's routine. She bustled back into the room after we had been there an hour, announcing 'naptime' for Zelda and herding us out of the sitting room. Zelda pouted and poured herself another whisky.

'You never let me have any fun.'

'We'll come again, I promise,' said Miles. 'I'd love for you to tell me tall tales about the Brighton Coven.'

'Please come soon. This old biddy here wants to make me live longer by removing all my vices. I keep telling her it will only seem longer.'

'Is it my fault I love you and don't want you to die?'

'Don't be silly, dear. We all die in the end. You can sell the flat and move to France with your girlfriend when I go.'

Diana turned puce, and her mouth worked, but no sound came out. I raised my eyebrows at the others, who jumped out of their seats.

'We've really got to go,' said Roz. 'My husband likes his dinner on the table at seven sharp.'

I turned a guffaw into a cough.

'Come on, Miles,' I said. 'We can't keep Ed waiting.'

We kissed Zelda's flaky powdered cheeks and thanked Diana who stood back, well out of social kissing range. She muttered 'good riddance' just loud enough for us to hear her as she shut us out of the flat.

'Did you get the feeling she wanted us to leave?' said Miles.

'I don't know what you mean.'

'I've got an idea,' said Roz. 'Natalee Hedges lives on the way home, on the outskirts of Shoreham. She's the one who told me about Blackwood. I'm sure she'll be able to help us with leads in this case.'

'I'm game if you are,' said Miles. 'Have you got an address for her?'

'Mouse will give us a postcode if we ask him,' I said. 'He's a whiz at finding people.'

Five minutes later, Miles had entered Natalee's postcode into his sat nav and we were heading towards a new housing estate. The presence of skips and piles of sand on the unfinished pavements showed just how new they were. Not a tree or a bush broke the profile of the concrete expanse, although some brave dandelions had flowered in the cracks between the walls and driveways.

We pulled up outside her house and headed for her front door. Miles kept his finger pressed on the doorbell until I felt forced to remove it.

'She might be asleep,' he said.

The door opened a crack on a chain, and I could see Natalee's pale face in the gloomy hallway.

'What do you want?' she said.

'You need to tell us about your relationship with Vivian Blackwood,' I said.

'Vivian? No, you've got it wrong. I couldn't. My husband… Oh my God.'

She sank to the floor, her head in her hands, whispering no, no, no. Roz took over.

'Natalee, It's Roz. You've got to help us. Somebody murdered Vivian, and you could be a suspect.'

Natalee's head came up from her knees.

'Roz? I wouldn't. I couldn't.'

'You must tell us what you know. The murderer is still out there, and they will kill again if we don't stop them,' said Miles.

'Please open the door,' I said.

'Okay, but you can't stay long. My husband doesn't like me to have guests when he's not here.'

Natalee showed us into her sitting room, and we all perched on the plastic-covered seats. The carpet looked new, and the coffee table gleamed. I couldn't see a single fingerprint on the glass. I felt as if we had entered a showroom. Natalee did not sit down. She wrung her hands together and glanced behind her, making me feel panicky. I nodded at Roz, who took the lead.

'The police are looking into Vivian's relationships,' said Roz. 'Since you introduced me to him, I thought you might be able to—'

'We weren't in a relationship,' said Natalee. 'Never. I would never. He found out about…'

'About what?' I said.

Natalee swallowed.

'It's confidential. You mustn't tell anyone. I'm leaving my husband. He's, um, difficult, and I need to get away from him. He'd stop me if he knew. Vivian found out and threatened to tell him if I didn't...'

'If you didn't what?' said Miles.

'Bring him new clients.'

'Like me?' said Roz.

'Yes, and Emily Carradine. He threatened me before he died because I told him I couldn't do it anymore.'

'Did you kill him?' I said.

'No. I wanted to, but I was so close to escaping this prison. I would never put myself in another one.'

'What will you do now?'

'I'm planning on leaving my husband in the next couple of weeks. I'm worried sick he might find out about my plans, and now...'

'And now what?' said Roz.

'Whoever killed Vivian might come for me next. Emily knows I was helping him. Who else might have found out? Vivian Blackwood was a blackmailer and a thief and preyed upon people at the lowest point in their lives. One of his clients must have had enough and got even. What if I'm on their list?'

'No one will blame you. You were being blackmailed too,' I said.

'You don't know that. People are irrational. You've got to go now. If you want to know who killed Vivian, you need to interview his clients first. Everybody hated him.'

'Who would you talk to?'

'Emily maybe, or Robin Huxley. Please leave. My husband could be here any minute.'

We all stood up and peeled ourselves off the plastic couches. I couldn't wait to get out of there, even though I had only spent a few minutes in that house. How could she tolerate it? No wonder she was leaving.

'You should go straight away,' said Roz. 'It's dangerous to stay with him.'

'I can manage a few more days. I need to get the monthly housekeeping money from him first, and then I'm leaving.'

'Be careful,' said Miles.

'I've been careful for years,' said Natalee. 'Now I'm going to start living again.'

'Give me your number. Just in case,' I said.

'You won't need it. Leave me alone. I can fight my own battles.'

Chapter 11

We drove in silence for the first few miles after leaving Natalee's house. I couldn't find anything sensible to say. Natalee seemed to have the situation under control, but her fear made me feel sick. To distract myself from thinking about her, I read the notes I had scribbled during our visit to Zelda. Sometimes, being a private detective is not so different from being a medium. You have only sparse information to work with, and you have to persuade people to tell you about things they intended to keep to themselves. Not that Zelda appeared to be hiding her actual feelings. From what she told us, there was no love lost between her and Blackwood, and I got the impression she nursed a deep disappointment about the way Blackwood used his undoubted gifts. I didn't have the gall to ask her what sort of medium she claimed to be. Her aura intimidated me, despite her infirmities.

One fact stood out from our visit to Zelda. Blackwood had never learned to hypnotise people, so how did he garner the specific pieces of information he used to convince any sceptical clients? I remembered the shocked expression on Roz's face when he mentioned Vinnie at the seance. How had he known to use that name? It's not exactly common. I tapped her on the shoulder.

'Are you sure you didn't tell Blackwood your mother called you Vinnie?'

'Positive.'

'So how did he know?'

She shrugged.

I couldn't understand it. From what Zelda had told us, the vast majority of mediums were 'open eye' and relied on their senses to pick up the clues scattered by their clients. They also used the desperation of people who latched on to the simplest prompt. By telling a room of ten people somebody whose name began with A or P wanted to talk to them, you could almost guarantee someone would tell you their maternal Grandfather was called Peter. And if you asked, 'Are you sure it's him? What did he look like?'; you could get them to tell you he was plump with a pince-nez. Then you could confirm it was him and add a detail like a waistcoat, because the chances were high he would be wearing one. And so on. While I could imagine that sort of trick fooled most people receptive to anything that might assuage their grief, Roz Murray could not be fobbed off with cheap party tricks. Knowing her nickname meant either he had a direct line to her mother or… I let out a gasp.

'What is it?' said Miles. 'Have you had an insight into the identity of the killer?'

'No, but I've had an idea. I need to go straight home and talk to Mouse.'

'What about the shop?' said Roz.

'It can stay closed until tomorrow. Who's going to notice?'

Miles dropped me at my car, and I drove around town doing errands before completing a massive shop at the supermarket. I almost fainted at the cash register when they told me the total. The primary culprit was Hades's premium cat food, which had risen in price again, but he wouldn't eat anything else and would go on hunger strike if I bought the cheaper brands. I paid up. What choice did I have? At least we had a local vet who didn't belong to a franchise. If Hades got ill, we wouldn't have to mortgage the house. I couldn't get rid of him, but his residence was hanging by a thread every time he acted like the Queen of Sheba.

The traffic crawled back through Seacastle from the supermarket. It took almost as long to get home as it had taken to come back from Brighton. I texted Mouse to come and help me unpack the groceries when I got home, as I didn't have a hope of carrying them all by myself. He was waiting outside with Harry when I finally arrived, so I didn't have to take anything indoors.

Mouse could hardly contain himself when he heard I had been to see Zelda Romano. He'd been reading about her on the internet and had been seriously impressed by her reputation.

'Did she try to read your aura?' he said. 'I bet it was spooky being in the same room as her.'

'Actually, she drinks whisky and smokes like a chimney, so her flat reminded me of the Shanty in the days before smoking got banned.'

'I can never believe people used to smoke in bars and clubs.'

'And offices,' said Harry.

'And aeroplanes,' I said. 'Long-haul flights were murder.'

'Did Zelda tell you anything useful about Blackwood?' asked Harry.

'She told us that nearly everyone he ever met wanted to kill him.'

'That doesn't narrow the field much.'

'And that he couldn't hypnotise people. It's a matter of opinion whether he qualified as a medium at all. He had no clairvoyant ability and couldn't communicate with the dead. He was a con man who read his victims like open books.'

'Hear me out,' said Harry. 'Isn't that what his clients wanted? Didn't they want assurance their loved ones were okay? Didn't he provide a service?'

'Harry's right. Roz got much better after Blackwood pretended he could communicate with her mother,' said Mouse.

'If that was all he did, we wouldn't be investigating his murder,' I said.

'That's true. He had some sort of racket going. He's hard to pin down, and I have tried. I need a breakthrough, and then all will be revealed.'

'George has ordered a trawl through his financials. I'm willing to bet the house he'll find malfeasance and blackmail in every line of the bank statements,' I said.

'If he didn't use hypnosis, how did he find out people's secrets to begin with?' said Harry.

'Could he have shared information about clients with other mediums? That's how M Lamar Keene did it,' said Mouse.

'And who's he?' asked Harry.

'A medium who nearly got assassinated for revealing his methods,' said Mouse. 'I read about him today.'

'Miles had heard of him too. It hasn't stopped people from believing they can communicate with the dead. You reminded me of an idea I had in the car on the way home from Brighton. Maybe Blackwood used some sort of bugging or electronic listening devices to listen in on people's private conversations?'

'But how would he get people to carry them around?' said Harry.

'What if Titania is his accomplice? I saw her fiddling with Roz's phone while Roz was in the seance. Could she have added some sort of software or app to Roz's phone?'

'Unlikely,' said Mouse. 'The hardware would be too bulky to hide inside a phone case. In theory, Titania could have installed some sort of spyware on the phones, but only the Android ones. Apple phones would be impossible to crack. Also, any spyware would cause the battery to drain and performance to plummet. People would notice the difference immediately and might get a technician to check. Any decent tecky guy would spot the spyware immediately.'

'Why don't we check Roz's phone?' I said.

'You mean me? I can examine it if you like. If Titania installed anything, I'll know.'

'I think we should question Titania about Blackwood's methods. Can you help me, as I wouldn't know what to ask her?'

'Sure. Why don't you tell her to come to the shop for coffee tomorrow? Pretend you found a gothic piece in one of your clearances she might like.'

'I doubt she'll want to talk to us, but it's worth a try.'

Chapter 12

The next morning, I received a group text from Ghita alerting me about a step class being held in the church hall. As well as being a fabulous cook and a standout friend, Ghita ran the Fat Fighters Club, which George referred to as the 'fat fighters' in his un-woke manner. He had a point. We were all over forty, many with menopausal weight gain, and nobody ever lost a pound, not that they were questioned about their diets. People attended the classes for their fast pace, eighties soundtrack and post-exercise coffee and cake, or a pint in the Shanty, with the chance to catch up on Seacastle gossip, depending on what time the class finished. Most people were serial attendees and tended to be members of our friend group, but occasionally we had onetime drop-ins or the friend of a friend. Normally Roz would come to these classes, but she had gone to sea with Ed. When I texted a confirmation, Ghita rang me back.

'I hear you and Roz have fallen out. That makes a change. Usually, it's me and Roz that aren't speaking. What on earth did you fight about? She was furious with you.'

'Vivian Blackwood, but we made up. We're friends again.'

'You can tell me all about it after class tonight. I'm doing a shift at the council today. They rang me up and asked if I would consider coming back full time for a while as they are short-handed because one of the planning gals is pregnant.'

'That's great. Will you go full time?'

'Not for now. Don't worry, you'll still have my help, and I'll bake cakes for Second Home. It might be worth training someone else up, though.'

'It doesn't bear thinking about. I'm really looking forward to the class tonight. My flab has rolls.'

'Ha! We're all like butterballs at the moment. Remind me to tell you about Craig Latchford, by the way.'

'Craig Latchford? Why?'

'I think he may have had dealings with Blackwood.'

'You just reminded me. I met him outside Blackwood's building.'

'Seriously? Well, we need to talk in that case. See you tonight.'

After Ghita rang off, I packed my exercise bag with shoes and assorted pieces of Lycra to take to the shop with me. I loved Ghita's classes. Even thinking about them put a spring in my step for the rest of the day. I left a note for Mouse on the kitchen table in case he fancied coming too, but he probably wouldn't. Ghita loved Mouse, but he distracted the ladies with his Prince Charming looks and lazy smile. He didn't even do it on purpose. I wondered what Ghita knew about Craig

Latchford. We had been so concentrated on Blackwood's clients as potential murderers I had completely forgotten about bumping into him.

I had a busy day in the shop, made busier by the absence of my two helpers. Mouse arrived for the lunchtime rush and spent the whole time upstairs in Second Home, charming people into having another slice of cake to take home or a second latte. That boy is a born salesman. As I was taking a breather on my stool behind the cash register, Miles Quirk came into the shop wearing a green ensemble that gave him the appearance of a lost leprechaun.

'Hello again. Long time no see.' His eyes twinkled when he spotted Mouse upstairs. 'Hasn't he grown?' he said, tugging at his cravat. 'Such a handsome young man.'

'And me?'

'Yes, well, dear. We can't be young forever, can we?'

I felt like punching him in the nose, but I smiled sweetly.

'Since you're obviously not here to rain compliments down on my person,' I said. 'To what do I owe the pleasure of this visit so soon after our jaunt to Brighton?'

He smirked.

'The chairs in the window display,' he said. 'You could do so much better.'

I pursed my lips.

'Would you like to rearrange them?' I said. 'My window designer is on holiday.'

'No, that's okay. I'm going to take them off your hands anyway. And the Formica table too, if you give me a good price. I have a client who has been searching for that ensemble for months.'

'Really? I'm afraid they're reserved.'

'Reserved? They can't be.'

His expression went from smirking to crestfallen in an instant. I almost felt sorry for him. Still, it served him right. I let him mourn for a full five minutes before I told him I might let him have them at a premium. He paid up too. I couldn't believe my luck.

'Did you hear any more about that medium fellow?' he said as I tapped the numbers into my card reader.

'Not since yesterday. Have you?'

'No, but I had forgotten that my friend Noreen lives on the same floor as Blackwood's flat. She's got ears like a bat, and she is very knowledgeable about our Mr Blackwood.'

'Really? And has she told you what she knows?'

'Me? Oh Lord no. I'm no gossip. But she might tell you if I introduced you. You know how I love a thorough investigation.'

I rolled my eyes at him. Miles never met a double entendre he didn't flog like a dead horse.

'I am still doing some digging if you genuinely want to help. What's her name?'

'Noreen Ashcroft. She's a wealthy widow I met at an antique fair. I find special pieces for her collection. She's trying to spend her dead husband's entire fortune before she goes to join him.'

'Did she speak to her husband through Blackwood?'

'Good heavens, no! Her husband would die again if he knew how much money she had frittered away. She loves a Caribbean cruise. She used to go with her Pomeranian, Lord Fluffy, but he died. I suspect she tried to contact the dog using Blackwood once, but she won't talk about it. She can be quite difficult.'

I laughed. Miles Quirk could be highly amusing as well as extremely irritating. Meeting Noreen Ashcroft sounded like lots of fun and possibly a source of information about Blackwood's foibles.

'When can we go?'

'How about tomorrow afternoon? I'll give her a tinkle and make sure she'll be in. I recommend you take her some of Ghita's delicious lemon biscuits. She loves a sweet treat.'

'Can you text me the time of the meeting?'

'Of course. Is it possible to have these chairs and table delivered? I don't have transport for them right now. I had a row with the van company.'

The least surprising thing about Miles Quirk was the number of feuds he had running at any one time. The man could be insufferable.

'Harry will do it for you. Just text me the address and time and we'll get them to you.'

'Thank you. I'll see you tomorrow. Can you wear something less gauche? I really can't be seen with you dressed like that.'

Before I had a chance to reply, he had sashayed out of the door and minced down the street. He never changed. He could be adorable one moment and acidic the next, like a sherbet bomb.

'How can you stand him?' said Mouse, coming downstairs. 'He's like a colourful viper.'

'He's not so bad when you get to know him. He's predictable, at least. If he says something nice to you, you can guarantee he's about to insult you next. Are you coming to Ghita's class?'

'I'd like to, but she always gets cross with me.'

'Why don't you and I stand in the back? I can protect you from the dirty old ladies if you take the step beside the side wall.'

'Okay. Let's do that. I love her classes. I can boogie all I want with no one judging me.'

Chapter 13

We arrived at the church hall to find it had not been cleared for Ghita's class. A circle of plastic chairs left over from the latest meeting of Alcoholics Anonymous sat in the centre of the room. Several leaflets lay abandoned on the floor, as if someone had given up and dropped them there after realising they weren't ready yet. Other chairs that had been scattered around the hall had been moved to give passage to the coffee table and the entrance. The musty odour of smelly socks and cigarettes made my nose wrinkle. Ghita stood with her hands on her hips, surveying the rows of chairs with her eyebrows drawn together.

'Honestly. I pay to use the hall, you know. Wouldn't you think they'd clear it for me?'

Actually, knowing how much she paid, I thought she was lucky to have it at all, but I tutted and shook my head anyway.

'It won't take long with three of us,' said Mouse.

Ghita frowned.

'Are you taking the class tonight? Stay at the back. I don't want you distracting my ladies.'

Since some of them attended merely on the off-chance Mouse would turn up too, that seemed a little harsh.

'Let's get on with it,' I said and winked at Mouse.

Working together, we stacked the plastic chairs against the back wall in no time. We also reached the high-level windows with a broom and opened the catches to let a cooling breeze percolate through the stuffy atmosphere. Several gigantic spiders were reluctant to leave and lingered on the parquet floor. Mouse persuaded them to relocate under the stacked chairs with the same broom. Ghita set up her boombox and gave Mouse a plastic bag full of CDs. He looked at the defunct technology with disgust.

'Who even plays these anymore?' he said.

'Do your worst,' she said. 'We need something fast-paced with a heavy beat.'

As befitted a young man brought up in the internet age, Mouse asked ChatGPT which disc would be best suited for a step class. Apparently, AI likes to get down with Funky Town – 20 Classic 80s Dance Hits. Who knew? He handed it to Ghita who nodded in approval.

'I hope everyone took their vitamins this morning, because we are going to rock this joint,' she said, wobbling her head in approval.

She shoved the CD into the slot and turned up the volume. The opening bars of Jump (for my love) filled the church hall. A woman entering the hall dropped her water bottle in fright, and it rolled around on the floor as she scrambled to retrieve it. She was followed by the other members of the Fat Fighters club in various attires, from serious Lycra get-ups to a mere change of shoes and hair thrust into a bun. Ghita favoured a one-piece black Lycra worn over black-and-white striped tights.

She resembled a manic bumblebee bouncing from flower to flower as she did her warmup. Some women had congregated in the centre of the hall. From the fragments of conversation I picked up, I realised they were discussing the death of Vivian Blackwood. One woman, whom I didn't recognise, seemed to lead the discussion. I elbowed my way into the group to hear better.

'How'd he do it? That's what I'd like to know.'

'He tried to blackmail us, but we weren't having it. Her mother's sister-in-law's brother said Blackwood wasn't who he claimed to be, and he had dirt on people, which he tried to use against them. Blackwood changed his name more than once. He wasn't even a proper medium. He used to call himself—'

'Ladies! Ladies! Can you please take your places? Remember, the class lasts forty-five minutes so please pick a step height you can manage for the whole time.'

The woman muttered to herself, annoyed at being cut off at the climax of her revelation. She wasn't the only one. I stomped to the back of the hall where Mouse had laid out my yoga mat and step beside his set.

'People who eavesdrop never hear good of themselves,' he said, wagging his finger at me.

'Actually, she was just getting to the good part. She said Blackwood changed his name and wasn't always a medium. Don't let her leave without my speaking to her.'

Mouse sighed.

'Can you please forget about the case for five minutes and have some fun with me?'

'You're the one who encouraged me to investigate.'

He grinned.

'I'd forgotten that part.'

'No talking down the back! Let's go. Marching on the spot with your knees high, everyone.'

Ghita gave us a fake glare, and we were off. Soon, menopausal panting was the only sound in the hall besides the punchy music. Mouse hardly broke a sweat, but his enjoyment showed on his face. He loved dancing. I wished both he and Ghita could find a partner in the dance of life. Someone who made them glow as much as the step class. I almost crashed to the floor face-first as I caught my toe on my step. Mouse caught me and saved me from the face-plant.

'Concentrate on the class,' he said.

I didn't bother explaining I had not been thinking about the murder. By the time we finished the class, most of us were on our last legs. It took me a good minute or two to get my breath back and lift myself off my mat. I scanned the room for the woman who had such strong opinions about Blackwood. To my annoyance, she had slipped out without staying to help replace the chairs, not that I blamed her for that. I dashed outside, but she had vanished.

I returned indoors and helped with bad grace. Soon the hall had been returned to its habitual state, and the spiders were heading back to their territories, muttering about noisy humans scaring away the flies. I made Mouse wait while I nipped into the bathroom to wash my hands and redo my lips. The church loos were tiny and claustrophobic, and the water which issued from the taps scalded my hand. I swore under my breath and dried my hands on my sweaty t-shirt. I could hardly see myself in the foxed mirror as I leant in to reapply my lipstick. I heard the squeak of a cubicle door behind me, and the missing woman emerged, in a new outfit, still red-faced with exertion.

'Blimey,' she said. 'There's not enough room to swing a cat in here.'

She squeezed past me, bumping me with her gym bag, and went to wash her hands.

'Be careful. The water's boiling,' I said.

'Oh, thanks love. Honestly, why does it need to be hot at all?'

'I don't know,' I said, smiling at her in the mirror. 'I heard you talking about that medium fellow earlier. Did you know him?'

She looked startled.

'No, I didn't. I'm not the sort to hang around with criminals. I've got to go. My lift's waiting.'

'But I'd like to speak to your mother's sister-in-law's brother about what he knows, if that's possible.'

I gave her a pleading look, but she sneered at me.

'Who are you? You don't look like a copper, but you sound like one. I'm no nark. You won't get any answers out of me.'

She pushed past me and out of the bathroom. I didn't have the courage to follow her out. I shouldn't have blurted out the stuff about her relation. Only an interfering busybody would remember that sort of detail, or a copper. I found Mouse waiting beside the Mini.

'What kept you?' he said. 'I saw the woman you wanted to talk to leave just now. She looked as if she were having a major strop.'

'That's my fault. I put my enormous foot in it. I don't suppose you copied the number plate of her car?'

'Don't be ridiculous. We're not in the movies. The back window had a sticker on it, though. Something about a tennis club.'

'That's not much help. We'll have to leave it for now. Let's take the car home and then bring Harry to the Shanty for a pint in a taxi. We can eat one of their delicious pies.'

'They've become even more delicious since Gladys helped Joy with the recipes. We can't stay late. Aren't you going to see Miles Quirk's old lady tomorrow?'

'Thank goodness you reminded me.' I scratched my head. 'We're still at square one with this investigation. Blackwood's no saint, but so far we don't have any motive to kill him.'

'Beside Antrim's.' said Mouse.

I frowned at him.

'Terry did not kill Vivian Blackwood. Somebody knows something, and we'll soon get some leads to the actual killer.'

'That woman had one thing right. It's not as if he's a genuine medium,' said Mouse. 'Am I allowed to tell you what I found out about him now you're investigating?'

'Probably.'

Ghita came over to us, shaking her head.

'I hope you weren't harassing one of my ladies. It's hard enough to fill the class already.'

'She might have important information about the case.'

'And what about me? Have you forgotten I have the skinny on Councillor Latchford? According to the Seacastle Herald, he had business dealings with Blackwood, and he's a most unsavoury character.'

'Craig Latchford?' said Mouse.

'I forgot to tell you I met him at the seance,' I said. 'I didn't realise he might be important. Do you want to come to the Shanty with us, Ghita, and spill the beans while eating a most savoury pie?'

'I'll get my coat.'

Chapter 14

There are few more welcoming places than the Shanty pub on the outskirts of town. Despite its awkward location, the pub is popular with a fiercely loyal clientele. The owners/managers, Ryan and Joy Wells, made it feel like home from home with its seaside decor and tasty menu. They had been through tough times recently, and the people of Seacastle had responded by increasing their visits and their spend at the venue. Joy had blossomed since she had found her mother, Gladys, who couldn't stop smiling. Ryan surveyed the fun from his high-tech wheelchair. He loved to tinker with it and add to its already amazing selection of functions. When he worked behind the bar, he raised the seat so he could serve people with ease and be on the same level as his clients.

We got out of the taxi in the car park and wandered along the cliff-top path to the door of the pub. Ed Murray's boat lay at anchor in Pirate's Harbour below us, and the white horses in the bay ran in through the entrance and dissolved into the clear waters. The moon had already risen in the still blue sky, and the craters showed clearly on its battered surface. Mouse stopped to take a few deep breaths and stare out to sea.

'How could I live anywhere else?' he said.

Ghita stood on tiptoe to give him a hug, her cherub face still pink with exertion from giving the class. I beamed at her over his shoulder.

'Come on, you two. All the pies will be gone.'

Harry had arrived before us and taken possession of our favourite table in the window nook at the back of the pub. He had a half-finished pint of Guinness in front of him and a creamy moustache as evidence of the fate that had befallen the first half. I stopped at the bar to order food and drinks for the four of us and to have a chat with Ryan. His whole being had relaxed since they had now retired from service with the government. I wondered if he missed the thrill of their clandestine trips to Europe, but I didn't want to break the mood by asking. Instead, we discussed the forthcoming concert by a well-known local group that specialised in sea shanties.

'Joy certainly has an eclectic taste in music,' I said.

'And in men. Look at me,' said Ryan, laughing.

'She likes them brainy. I prefer muscle.'

'Don't let Harry hear you say that,' said Mouse, who was listening in. 'Harry thinks he could go on Mastermind.'

Ryan scratched his head.

'There's nothing to stop him from appearing on the show, but would he get any of the questions right?'

'Only if his speciality subject was the history of pies,' I said.

'That's mean,' said Mouse. 'Harry knows a load about all sorts of stuff, just not intellectual things.'

'And I have excellent taste,' I said. 'So he must be doing something right.'

'If you have excellent taste, how come you married my Dad?' said Mouse.

'The folly of youth.'

Ryan grinned.

'George isn't that bad,' he said. 'Your sister likes him.'

'Touché,' I said. 'Let me know when the food order is ready.'

Ghita had already made her way to the table and was telling Harry about the step class with the concentration of a fanatic. His eyes had begun to glaze over when we rescued him from the deluge of detail.

'Ghita tells me you ambushed a poor woman in the car park,' he said.

'Not exactly. I heard her talking about the murder of Vivian Blackwood. It sounded as if she had important information about him. I tried to talk to her, but she drove off.'

'And called you a copper,' said Mouse.

'Ah, it might be tricky to get any sense out of her now she thinks you're connected with the police.'

'I'm still going to track her down. She can talk to George if she won't talk to me.'

'When is someone going to ask me about Craig Latchford?' said Ghita. 'I don't want to say I told you so when George handcuffs him.'

'You think he murdered Blackwood?' asked Harry.

'He's definitely the prime suspect in my eyes, but no one ever listens to me.'

'I'm listening,' said Ryan. 'And I'm much cleverer than them, so you must have a point.'

'Thank you. Anyway, as I was saying—'

'Who ordered the fish pie?' said Shaylah, staggering under the weight of her tray.

Ghita rolled her eyes but smiled anyway.

'Me, thanks.'

'Mine's the steak and ale,' said Mouse.

'And mine,' said Harry.

'Chicken and leek for me,' I said. 'Have you got any ketchup?'

'Course,' said Shaylah. 'Wouldn't fit on the tray, would it? I'll be back.'

She walked to the bar with the enthusiasm of a prisoner walking to the gallows and picked up the ketchup, examining the label as if she had never seen it before.

'Honestly,' said Ghita. 'Do you think she does it on purpose?'

'Absolutely,' said Mouse. 'Come on, tell us about the councillor.'

Ghita pursed her lips and waited for Shaylah to sashay over and dump the ketchup bottle on the table.

'She has such a lovely way about her,' I said to Ryan who corpsed.

'It's hard to get good staff around here,' he said.

'Impossible by the looks of it,' said Harry, making Mouse giggle.

'Don't be mean,' said Ryan. 'She's still traumatised after finding a body outside the pub. I had to give her a raise.'

'The more you pay her, the grumpier she gets. Maybe cut her salary and see if that works?'

'I don't want to be the next body,' said Ryan.

'Can I please tell you about Craig Latchford now?' said Ghita.

'Okay, but not with your mouth full,' I said.

She pouted and swallowed her food, almost choking in her haste to speak. She washed it down with a mouthful of her drink and cleared her throat.

'Craig Latchford's a prime suspect, if you ask me. He worked as a councillor during my time in procurement and like most people, I avoided him when I could. He had a habit of asking for favours in different departments, most of which broke with protocol and standard practice. If he didn't get what he wanted, he could turn nasty. After one particularly dodgy scheme involving planning permission for the back garden of his mother's bungalow, the council hauled him in and forced him to resign.'

'What's he doing now?' asked Harry.

'Rumour has it, he's trying to get elected again. There's a seat that may become vacant soon as the incumbent is unfortunately unwell and not expected to recover sufficiently to carry on.'

'But what's that got to do with Blackwood?' I said.

'I'm not sure. But Roz told me Latchford used to frequent Blackwood's premises. Supposedly he was trying to contact his father, a decorated war hero.'

'Supposedly?' said Harry.

'Latchford's father worked for British Rail,' said Mouse, waving his tablet. 'It's all here on the internet.'

'Why would he lie?' I said.

'He liked to big himself up,' said Ghita. 'But what if he needed Blackwood for other reasons?'

'That's fascinating,' said Ryan. 'But I can't see why he would murder Blackwood?'

'Well, that's not my job,' said Ghita, colouring. 'Tanya's the one who figures out who killed whom and why. I just bake cakes and drive middle-aged women to exhaustion.'

'You're brilliant at both things,' said Mouse. 'Your class today was epic!'

'Thanks,' she said. 'I know, but I can't help thinking I'm missing out somehow.'

'That's because Harry is stealing mouthfuls of your pie,' said Ryan. 'By the way, I'd love you to help Joy and Gladys with new flavours if you get the chance.'

'Just try and stop me.'

Chapter 15

The next morning, Harry and I left Seacastle under grey skies, heading west in our van along the coast. I inserted a cassette into our ancient player and turned up the volume. Harry grinned.

'Lynyrd Skynyrd? You rarely play that one.'

'I don't know why I chose it. It's one of my favourites. I'm nostalgic after Sarah's funeral. My mother loved Lynyrd Skynyrd.'

'Really? I had her down as a Frank Sinatra fan.'

'She liked him too, but I caught her playing my Skynyrd LP one afternoon when I came home early from school. She claimed it helped her complete boring tasks like the ironing, but she hadn't been ironing, and she was out of breath.'

'Dancing?'

'I don't know. Pink-cheeked with embarrassment though.'

'Why didn't she admit to liking it?'

'I'm not sure. Not part of her image. She always had much more in common with my sister than with me.'

'Helen is quite retro. Maybe you should try to sell her in your shop; rare vintage housewife.'

'Don't even consider telling her that. We don't share the same sense of humour either.'

'I noticed.'

We drove in silence for a while, and I gazed out of the window at the summer hedges gleaming green in the damp air, laden with buds and early seed pods. We had to stop the van to allow a large flock of sheep to cross the road, swinging their fat tails and bleating to each other. An elderly collie followed them, nipping at their heels, watched by a young dog who gambolled about without helping. The farmer grabbed his collar as we drove past, and he barked hysterically at the van as it sped away.

'Are we nearly there yet?' I said.

'It's in the next village. Keep an eye out for a pub called The Highwayman.'

'We're clearing a pub?'

'No, the cottage next door to it. The owner, Polly Bridges, told me she'd meet us at the bar.'

'Excellent. I'm dying to pee. We can have a coffee before we get started.'

We parked the van in the space between the pub and the tumbledown cottage next door. The outside of the cottage did not encourage me, but experience had taught me never to prejudge a clearance from the appearance of the house. The interior of the pub had recently been redecorated, and every trace of character had been surgically removed. Even the bar stood shiny in Chrome and faux marble. An odour of gloss paint hung in the air. Instead of chairs, square blocks covered in various shades of beige were scattered around tables of smoky glass. The look on Harry's face told me his opinion of the new décor.

'Well, this is different,' I said, cutting him off with his mouth open and approaching the young woman standing at the bar.

'I decorated it myself,' she said. 'Well, I had help, but you know what I mean.'

'I certainly do,' said Harry, catching my eye.

'It's striking,' I said. 'And you also own the cottage next door?'

'Yes, it belonged to my aunt.'

'It's such a pretty home,' I said.

'Do you think so? I suppose old people like that sort of thing.'

Old people? What a cheek! I tried not to react. Maybe she meant her aunt.

'They do,' I said. 'A picturesque cottage never goes out of fashion.'

'Especially if it's right beside a pub,' said Harry.

'Will you empty it?' said the young woman. 'I want to get the decorators in as soon as possible.'

I considered advising her to leave some original features if she wanted to sell it, but my spirit rebelled. She'd soon find out for herself, and I was pretty sure I'd be dissed for any advice I offered her.

'Generally, we only take anything that we can offload later,' said Harry. 'But we can clean it out if you pay us.'

'I'll pay you two hundred pounds in cash. You can use the brooms from the pub.'

'Make it three hundred and it's a deal.'

She pouted.

'Two fifty, and not a penny more.'

Harry rubbed his chin.

'It's a deal,' he said, extending his hand, which she ignored.

'The brooms are in there,' she said, pointing behind the bar.

I followed the direction of her finger and discovered a couple of dodgy brooms in a cupboard. They were semi-bald but were still serviceable. I didn't comment on their state; instead I grinned.

'Any chance of a coffee?'

'The barman isn't in yet. You can buy a can of something at the local shop if you are thirsty.'

I swallowed the response that bubbled up in my throat. Oblivious, she fished around in her handbag and took out a roll of fifty-pound notes. She peeled off five notes and handed them to Harry, who raised an eyebrow at me.

'Let's go,' he said.

The cottage sat back from the road in a garden filled with herbs and hollyhocks. Dog roses crawled up the white-washed walls and invaded the eaves. Swifts darted in and out of nests clinging to the underside of the roof. Greying lace curtains hung behind the windows. I could almost picture the spiders' webs in the corners of the ceilings. Harry twisted the doorknob and pushed open the door, dislodging the pile of junk post underneath the letterbox. I picked up a leaflet offering cheap cremation plans.

'I think they may be too late,' I said.

As my eyes adjusted to the gloom, I realised we had entered the house of a herbalist of some sort. The passageway was lined with narrow shelves filled with glass bottles with mysterious contents.

'Wow! I can sell these at auction,' I said. 'Where do you think the loo is?'

'Upstairs, or maybe in the back garden?'

I crossed my fingers I would find it upstairs, but unfortunately I spotted a shed through the window, at the end of the narrow garden, slumped to one side like a disappointed suitor. I sighed in resignation and pulled a tissue from my pocket.

'Wish me luck,' I said to Harry, as I pulled open the back door, which creaked loudly in protest.

The humming of bees filled the air as I made my way down the overgrown path to the outside toilet. A smell of honeysuckle permeated the air, and I breathed it in grateful for the bounty of nature. The privy had definitely seen better days. I couldn't believe the previous owner had never felt the need to replace it. Perhaps she couldn't afford it. I pushed cautiously at the door, and then pulled instead, as it remained tightly shut. Harry watched me from the back door and strode over to help me when he saw me struggle.

'How long has she been dead?' he said. 'This door is stuck fast.'

But it wasn't stuck. It had been nailed shut. Harry heaved on it, and the frame came away from the wall with the door.

'Oops. I don't suppose it matters. They're sure to install a bathroom in the cottage when they do it up.'

I peeped into the shed, expecting the worst. Apart from a few spiderwebs, it seemed to be clean and dry. A sturdy cardboard box with a lid balanced on top of the toilet bowl.

'What on earth's that doing in here?' I asked.

'Search me. Let me take it to the house, and you can get on with your business.'

Harry picked up the box and carried it down the path. I didn't bother trying to shut the door again.

When I had finished, I nipped back inside the house, my curiosity piqued by the box and its contents. I found Harry sitting at the kitchen table, reading a document with rapt attention.

'That's our day finished,' he said, handing it to me.

The heading on the document told me all I needed to know. It read the Last Will and Testament of Nelly Bridges, the owner of the cottage. I skimmed the pages and gasped. Nelly had left the building and all its contents to The Cats' Protection Society and made it executor of her will. Her niece Polly would be apoplectic. I grinned at Harry.

'We'd better call the Cats' Protection shop. I still have their number from the time we rescued those cats from a house clearance.'

Harry shuddered. 'I remember. The entire house was covered in poo and fur. What about the niece? I've still got her money.'

'Oh, we can let them tell her the good news and give it back to her. Let's see if they can come now.'

I took out my phone and after a quick search found the number I had for the local branch. The person I spoke to gave me a number for the regional manager, who happened to be in Shoreham for the day. When David Langley heard where we were, and why I was calling him, he offered to come straight over.

'Isn't there an excellent gastropub there?' he said.

'The Highwayman?'

'No, they've ruined that one. There's a Duke of Sussex just down the road from you. Why don't we meet there in an hour? By the way, what were you doing in the house?'

'We came to do a clearance, but I guess that's cancelled now.'

'Why don't you take the pieces you would have chosen anyway? We will make plenty of money for the society from the sale of the cottage, and if you hadn't found the will before Nelly's niece, I doubt we would ever have known about it.'

'Okay. Thank you. See you in an hour.'

'He's coming? Great.'

'And he says we can still do the clearance.'

'Now that's a win-win. It's a pity we won't get to see Polly's face when she finds out about the cottage.'

'It's tempting to stay, but maybe we should avoid a confrontation. Things could turn nasty when she finds out what happened to her inheritance.'

'She deserves everything she gets,' said Harry.

'Or doesn't.'

We recovered a decent haul of vintage furniture from the cottage. Nothing earth-shattering, but plenty of saleable stock for Second Home. I also found a gorgeous Mouseman oak kitchen chair with the trademark mouse carved onto its leg. It had a strong patina left by hundreds of bottoms over the last hundred years. I imagined Nelly Bridges sitting in it to read one of her herbal books and felt comforted that it would go to a good home. My friend Grace Wong would take it off my hands for her upmarket antique shop, and we would both make a tidy profit.

David Langley, from Cats' Protection bought us a delicious pub lunch, and we drove back to Seacastle the long way to avoid crossing paths with Polly Bridges. She shouldn't blame us for finding the will, but I had a feeling she might. At least she wouldn't get the chance to wreck the cottage as well as the pub. Harry whistled as he drove home, a sure sign he felt content with our day. I wondered how Roz was coping after our trip to see Zelda. Perhaps she could find solace in the better times she had with her mother. Roz didn't have any brothers or sisters, and she only had her husband Ed for company. He spent most of his life offshore on his fishing boat, so she needed support. Ghita and I would have to support her past the worst of it.

Since it was still early, we drove by the shop and unloaded our bounty. I placed the Mouseman chair in the shop window where I knew Grace would spot it eventually. She always bought the items I selected with her in mind. I'm not sure which of us was psychic. I piled the rest of the items haphazardly on the floor, to wait for me to return and sort them out. We arrived home to find Mouse wearing my apron and exotic spicy odours permeating the air of the Grotty Hovel, my pet name for our terraced house. He had taken to cooking like a duck to water and often surprised us with delicious suppers when he came home on his holidays.

I almost tripped over Hades, our bad-tempered rescue cat, who wound himself around my ankles, purring loudly. I knew better than to reach down and stroke him. He enjoyed giving me a vicious scratch just for the hell of it. Hades yowled piteously at me.

'Don't listen to him,' said Mouse. 'He's eaten twice today already.'

'That smells fantastic,' said Harry. 'What are you cooking?'

'Beef stew and dumplings. I know it's out of season, but I found some stewing beef in the freezer, and I didn't think it would last until the winter.'

'Beware the Squander Bug,' said Harry.

'My mother would be proud,' I said. 'Speaking of mothers. Did Roz come in to work today?'

'No, only Ghita. We sold the Habitat chairs today. Did you find anything interesting at the cottage?'

'We certainly did,' said Harry. 'Let's serve up the supper and we'll tell you all about it.'

Chapter 16

The next morning, I went into the shop and looked around at the chaos. The furniture from the cottage had not been polished for years, and the tops had dried out in the sunlight. I got out my cleaning gear and buffed the tabletops and legs with beeswax. Grace turned up almost immediately desperate to buy the Mouseman I had left in the window display. I didn't expect such an instant result. She wasn't big on unannounced social calls despite having lived in Seacastle for several years. Being from Hong Kong, she liked to have an excuse to come in if she hadn't warned me first.

'I saw the fabulous farmer's chair in the shop window,' she said. 'Is it for me?'

'It depends on how rich you are.'

She laughed.

'I've got cash.'

'Excellent.'

'How is poor Roz doing?'

'Much better now. It was quite a blow.'

'We are all orphans now.'

'Except for me,' said Mouse, arriving from the Co-op with milk supplies.

'Ah, just in time to help Grace carry the chair up the High Street to the Asian Antique Emporium,' I said.

'Of course,' said Mouse.

'Can I keep Mouse for an hour or two?' said Grace. 'I need to move some heavy furniture around the shop and Max can't manage it by himself.'

'Of course,' I said.

'I need to look in on Goose this afternoon,' said Mouse. 'Do you mind if I don't come back?'

'Not at all. Have fun with the baby.'

Grace handed me a wad of cash, and they set out towards her shop. I knew Grace would double or treble the chair's price and sell it to one of their high-end clients who wouldn't be seen dead in my shop. That's how we both made money from the same chair. I put the cash into the register and filled in the sales column. Then I headed upstairs to make myself a cup of tea. I took my handbag with me so it couldn't be snatched from the counter by an opportunistic thief. I sat at the window table and made notes about the case. So far, the only actual suspect was still Terry Antrim. Natalee Hedges seemed to me to be in danger of becoming the second victim, rather than a murder suspect. I tried not to remember her frightened face, but it kept appearing in my mind's eye.

Then I heard someone enter the shop and a man's voice calling out.

'Shop!'

'Up here,' I answered, unwilling to go downstairs.

Heavy footsteps came up the steps. And a bald head appeared followed by a heavyset body. Craig Latchford. What did he want?

'Tanya isn't it? I hope you remember me. We met outside Vivian Blackwood's flat the day he died.'

'I remember it well. How can I help you? Are you looking to buy some vintage furniture?'

He looked about him, and his nose wrinkled in disgust. I could almost predict what he was going to say.

'I'm more of a modern furniture man myself. I like new stuff. Quality goods.'

'I see. So what brings you to Second Home? Would you like a coffee or tea?'

'I'll have a cuppa if you have builder's tea. I'm not one for these weird foreign flavours.'

I could have guessed that too. I smiled and made him a pot of tea. He spotted the cake cabinet.

'What sort of cake is that?'

'It's an orange drizzle cake. Would you like a slice?'

'Not lemon? Oh, I'm not sure I'll like it.'

'I'm sure you will.'

'Okay. I'll risk it.'

I watched as he bit into the cake and shut his eyes in ecstasy as the tangy drizzle hit his tongue.

'This is proper cake,' he said. 'Where do you buy them?'

'Oh, Ghita makes our baked goods,' I said.

'Ghita, but I thought she worked as an administrator.'

'She bakes too,' I said. 'She's multi-talented.'

'I was hoping to speak to her this morning. Only you said she helped you in the shop sometimes.'

'She should be in later. Was there anything in particular you wanted?'

'I'm hoping to build an estate outside Lancing. I thought we could talk about planning permission.'

I took a shot in the dark.

'I remember now. You told me you were working on something with Vivian Blackwood.'

He dropped his cup onto his saucer, splashing tea everywhere. I handed him some napkins, and he dabbed at his trousers, his face puce with panic.

'It's not true,' he said. 'I didn't tell you any such thing. You're making it up.'

'I'm pretty sure you did,' I replied. 'You told me he was helping you with a housing project. I presume it's the same one.'

Craig Latchford stood up.

'I don't know who told you this, but it's not true. Blackwood was a con man. I would never have worked with him. I have a reputation to think of.'

Some reputation. I smiled at him as if everything were normal.

'Well, if you have to go, that will be six pounds fifty,' I said.

He threw a ten-pound note on the table.

'Keep the change. You look as if you need it.'

'Shall I tell Ghita you called around?'

'Don't bother. I've got better things to do.'

He headed back downstairs without a backward glance. I could understand why Ghita considered him a suspect, but in truth, he didn't have a motive, or as far as I knew, an opportunity. He was just a conman, like Blackwood. No wonder they were pals. I dismissed him from my thoughts and continued writing notes about the case. I made a side note about him, but his presence at Blackwood's flat that day seemed to be coincidental. I had lain back on the window seat and was heading for a nap when the shop doorbell clanged below me again. I leant over the railings to see if a customer or a friend had come into the shop.

'Is that you, Roz?' I called down.

'Um, no, it's Raven Huxley.'

'Raven who?'

'Raven Huxley, the influencer. We met at Vivian Blackwood's office. I was researching an article about him.'

The influencer? I'm Tanya Bowe, the Vintage Guru. No, don't say that.

'Come on up. I'm having breakfast if you fancy something?'

'No thanks. I'm on a diet.'

A slight, dark-haired girl with fake eyebrows and purple lipstick came up the stairs. She glanced around before approaching me and giving me her hand to shake. Her skinny fingers made me wonder why on earth she imagined she needed a diet, but perhaps she meant gluten-free or something. I gestured at the seat opposite me.

'Please sit down.'

She pulled the chair out and examined it with care before parking her bottom on it.

'I don't like second-hand furniture,' she said. 'Like, it might be infested.'

With what she didn't say. I tried not to bristle with fury.

'Um, why are you here, Miss Huxley? It's obviously not to buy my wares,' I said, smiling.

The joke flew right over her head and out of the shop window to languish with the seagulls on the opposite roof. She did not return my smile. She pursed her lips and took out a tablet, which she tapped at for the next five minutes without speaking to me. Two can play at that game. I took a croissant out of the cabinet and ate it with undisguised relish as she had pretended not to want one.

'Wow. These are so delicious,' I said, wiping the crumbs off my Led Zeppelin t-shirt. 'You don't know what you are missing.'

She shot me a look I took to be hate, and I beamed back.

'Well, I'm quite busy today. I need to get on if you can't get to the point a little quicker.'

She gave me a 'don't you know who I am' glare, which I ignored. I stood up, pretending to have finished with her. She grabbed my sleeve.

'Wait. Don't leave. I need to speak with you. I heard you're literally investigating the death of Vivian Blackwood. Is that true, like?'

'Yes.'

'Have you got any suspects yet?'

'All his clients are suspects right now, including you.'

Her face! I wish I had captured her expression.

'Me? Why would I... like, seriously? You can't mean that.'

'Why not?'

'I had no reason. Like, I only went to his office to get an interview.'

I raised an eyebrow.

'That's what you say.'

'Listen. I was within my rights. He tried to blackmail my sister. I wanted to find out how he did it.'

'How he did what?'

'Read her mind, like literally read it. How is that even legal? That's why I wanted to interview him, but he totally refused. Like, full-on, shut me down. Called me a snowflake and sent me away.'

'Why did Blackwood try to blackmail your sister? Did she have any money?'

'As if. I don't think it's any of your business, actually.'

What a rude woman! Two can play at that game.

'I'm not sure if you've grasped the elements of investigation,' I said, with an icy tone. 'In order to find out who killed Vivian Blackwood, and why, I need to ask the key witnesses questions to establish a motive and opportunity for the crime.'

'Who've you questioned besides me?'

I heard myself repeating the mantra of the investigative journalist and to tell you the truth, she reminded me of some of the dodgy characters I had met while working on 'Uncovering the Truth'.

'That's confidential information. I'm not at liberty to divulge my sources.'

She clenched her jaw, and her pupils shrank to dots in her grey eyes. I thought she might bite me. I wondered if she had imbibed something for Dutch courage before coming to see me at the shop.

'Seriously? You're literally not going to tell me?'

I smirked. Before I could answer, the shop bell rang again, and a customer entered.

'Hello, anybody here? I'm in a hurry,' she said.

I put my finger up to signal to Raven to wait one minute and ran downstairs.

'I'll be back,' I said.

The customer wanted a price for the pair of vinyl-covered kitchen stools left over from the batch purchased by Miles Quirk. They were profit-only items.

'How about twenty quid for the pair?'

'I'll give you eighteen in cash,' she said, holding up a twenty-pound note.

'It's a deal.'

I gave her a two-pound coin in change, and she picked up a stool in each hand. A thump from the Vintage distracted me for a second.

'Are you sure you don't need help?' I asked.

'No thanks. My husband is waiting around the corner with the car.'

I thanked her again and held the door open for her. Raven pushed past me through the open door and into the street.

'Leaving so soon?' I said. 'I can't say it was a pleasure.'

She turned to me with narrowed eyes.

'You think you're so smart? Next time I suggest you use your phone for confidential information.'

She ran off, her hair streaming behind her. It took me a couple of seconds to register what she had said. I ran upstairs, my heart in my mouth, but I already knew. My notebook, which I had left on the table, pinned open by a couple of glasses, had disappeared. I ran back downstairs and looked up and down the High Street, but she had disappeared. I couldn't believe I had been stupid enough to leave her alone upstairs. She had stolen my notes about the case. What if she blogged about Natalee's connection to Blackwood? Natalee would be in terrible danger.

I grabbed my phone to call her, but then I remembered her refusal to give me her number. An icy chill ran up my back. I had to call in the cavalry. George! He would have a fit, but I had to tell him quickly. He could get Natalee out of her house and into safety before Raven blogged about her. Shame almost overwhelmed me. Some private investigator I was! I swallowed my pride and rang him immediately. A long silence followed my confession. Finally he said, 'Don't panic, Tan. I'll get Joe onto it. She stole private information from you. He can pick up Raven Huxley before she does any damage. It'll be all right.'

But it wasn't.

Chapter 17

When I didn't hear from George, I passed a restless night tossing and turning and irritating Harry. I didn't want to annoy George by checking on him, so I had to assume Joe Brennan had alerted Natalee and shut down Raven's blog or at least prevented her from publishing anything on it. Instead, I dressed with care for my meeting with Noreen Ashcroft. Despite my reluctance to kowtow to Miles's idea of style, I channelled my inner Grace Wong (his style icon) and wore a pair of burgundy trousers and a white embroidered shirt. Harry raised both eyebrows in shock when I came down the stairs for breakfast.

'Are you going to a job interview at the bank?' he said.

'Actually, Miles Quirk has promised to introduce me to Noreen Ashcroft, a rich widow with a connection to Blackwood, who lives in his building. He's fussy about my outfit.'

'Miles Quirk? For heaven's sake. Are you really being intimidated by that ridiculous wimp? You should wear a tracksuit and false eyelashes and be damned.'

'He's not ridiculous, just over the top. His wit is rather caustic, but he's actually rather kind underneath. He's an acquired taste.'

'A taste I'm unlikely to share. Have an interesting time. This Noreen Ashcroft sounds like a hoot.'

'That's one word for it. I'll let you know how it goes.'

'Are you going to the shop dressed like that? You'll terrify the clients. They'll think the prices have gone up.'

'Hilarious. Do you want a lift anywhere? I'm taking the Mini.'

'No thanks. I'll stay here and turf the Mouse out of his bed. A growing boy needs his breakfast.'

'I'm having a latte and a slice of cake.'

'That's rather decadent of you.'

'It goes with the clothes.'

He laughed, and I kissed him. It felt great, so I kissed him some more. If Mouse had not staggered downstairs, I might have got distracted from my mission.

'Get a room you two. It's too early for that sort of behaviour.'

'Or too late,' I said. 'See you later.'

'See you in the shop,' said Mouse. 'I won't be long.'

I parked the car on a side street and tried to stroll nonchalantly to the shop. My ankles wobbled from side to side the entire way, making me flail my arms to keep my balance. I looked up and noticed Rohan and Kieron killing themselves with laughter at the door of Surfusion. They came over to Second Home still giggling.

'Love the outfit,' said Rohan.

'Trés chic,' said Kieron, biting his lip.

'I've got a meeting,' I said, struggling to open the door and escape their teasing.

'Who are you meeting?' said Kieron. 'Nineteen-eighty?'

'Don't be mean,' said Rohan. 'Nineteen-ninety at least.'

'And I thought it was only Miles who imagined he ran Vogue. Don't you have anything better to do?' I asked.

'Miles Quirk? Oh no, this will never do,' said Kieron. 'Rohan, make sure she doesn't escape.'

He ran off down the street and disappeared into the Oxfam charity shop. I entered the shop, feeling mildly traumatised by their criticism, and picked up the post. Luckily, there were no further bills to worry me. I turned to Rohan.

'I'm having a coffee and a big slice of cake. Can I interest you in the same?'

'Ooh, yes, please. Kieron has me on a diet, but he's not here, is he?'

We nipped upstairs to the Vintage and switched on the coffee machine. Soon we were gossiping on the window seat, and I got rid of the evidence of Rohan's cake by hiding his plate under a cushion. The shop bell clanged on its spring, and Kieron came in swinging a plastic bag.

'Cooey. Shop!'

'We're upstairs, sweets.'

Kieron appeared in the café, flushed with triumph.

'Look what I found,' he said, pulling a retro, swirly patterned shirt from his bag.

'Well, that's revolting,' I said. 'How do you know it's the right size?'

'I'm a style guru, and I've had a good look. Try it on while I make myself a coffee. Have you been feeding Rohan again? Honestly, the crumbs in your moustache are a dead giveaway.'

'He didn't have any cake,' I said. 'They must be from breakfast.'

Rohan gave me a grateful glance. Kieron handed me the shirt, and I took it to the loo. I struggled out of the white shirt, which was truthfully a size too small and too tight across my bust. Then, I put on the shirt Kieron had found at Oxfam. To my surprise, and annoyance, it looked fabulous with the trousers. I shuffled out and did a twirl.

'Now that's better,' said Rohan. 'Even Miles can't complain about that shirt. Before you looked like something out of the Sound of Music.'

He laughed at his own joke, and I turned to Kieron.

'He ate a large slice of cake,' I said. 'Monstrous. His plate's behind the purple cushion.'

Kieron laughed.

'I think he's gorgeous at any weight. Can I have whatever he had too, please?'

When the men had left again, I sat at the reception desk and laboured through the accounts for a few hours. Mouse turned up for the lunchtime shift at the Vintage and did a double take when he saw my shirt.

'You've changed again? I have to admit, I wasn't that keen on the first shirt.'

'Is there nobody without an opinion about my outfit today?'

'Stop fussing. At least we noticed. Anyway, you look great now. Retro as hell. You match your shop.'

'Our shop.'

He beamed.

'Our shop.'

'Can you run it while I go to meet Miles please? Ghita may turn up eventually, but I'm not really sure.'

'No problem. I've got this. Good luck with the widow.'

I dashed out of the shop to the Mini, almost spraining my ankle in the process. I had a large blister on each heel at this stage, and the pain made me wince. The drive to Blackwood's building took only ten minutes, so I arrived in plenty of time. As I stepped out of the car, a stiff sea breeze caught my hair and threw it in the air. I caught Miles staring at me.

'You look like a retro Valkyrie,' said Miles. 'I approve.'

'I'm so glad,' I said.

The sarcasm went right over his head.

'Let's go. Noreen likes visitors to be punctual.'

We took the lift to the sixth floor and rang the doorbell of the flat opposite Blackwood's on the opposite side of the stairwell. The door opened on a chain and an old woman I recognised, wearing an embroidered kaftan and a silk turban, peered through the crack.

'Miles! So good of you to bring me a visitor.'

She shut the door again, and I could hear the chain rattling as she struggled to release the catch. A dog yapped continuously in the background. Noreen shuffled away from the door and tried to calm it down. Miles shifted from foot to foot.

'Open the door already, you old bat,' he muttered.

'I'd prefer her to control the dog first,' I said. 'I'm a little nervous around lapdogs since one jumped up and bit my face.'

The door opened, and a wrinkled, bony wrist emerged holding a dog's leash.

'Can you take Priscilla for a walk please, Miles? She needs to go poo-poo right now. Here's a bag.'

Miles's eyes opened wide, and he nodded no, but said yes. I hid my delight at his discomfort and beamed at Noreen.

'I'm so honoured to meet you,' I said. 'Miles has told me all about you.'

'All lies, I'm sure,' she said. 'Why don't you come in, dear?'

My triumph at being asked to enter faded as I took my first breath in Noreen's flat. The smell of dog urine almost knocked me over. She must have been immune to the smell after so many years of exposure.

'Can you take your shoes off please, dear?' she said. 'The carpets are antique. Persian, mostly.'

I swallowed. If it hadn't been for the filth, I'd have cried with relief at taking off my uncomfortable heels, but the thought of walking on the urine-soaked carpets made me feel nauseous. I noticed she wore a pair of industrial-build slippers.

'Do you have an extra pair of slippers please? My socks are full of holes. I wouldn't feel comfortable taking off my shoes.'

She tutted but reached behind the door and produced an ancient pair of men's slippers, no doubt belonging to her deceased husband.

'I don't think they're haunted,' she said, thrusting them at me.

I put them on with great care to avoid falling over and touching the carpet. Then, I followed her over to the balcony. To my relief, we were sitting out in the sea air, and a strong breeze removed the lingering smells coming from the flat. She had made a pot of Earl Grey and placed some dodgy-looking sandwiches with curling edges on a cracked plate in the centre of the rattan table. A large fly landed on one of them and licked it with its prehensile tongue. I averted my eyes and accepted a cup of tea with no milk. I had a feeling it wouldn't be fresh either, and I couldn't face lumps in my tea. Noreen sipped hers and gave me a malevolent glance over the brim.

'Miles tells me you play at being detective,' she said. 'Are you any good at it?'

'I have worked with the police on several investigations,' I said, refusing to be drawn. 'I wouldn't call myself a detective.'

'Neither would I. You might be useful, though. I presume you want to understand the victim if you're here with me?'

'Miles tells me you knew him.'

'Knew of him would be more accurate, although I visited him once or twice to use his powers to contact dear departed Mr Fluffy.'

'Didn't I see you at the seance last week?'

She ignored the question, glaring at me through narrowed eyes.

'And did he get through to Mr Fluffy?' I said, trying again.

'Of course not. The man was a charlatan. His faculty for communicating with the dead could be compared to my husband's talent at preventing me from emptying his bank accounts. Futile and embarrassing.'

She stared off into the distance with a smirk on her face. A knock on the door interrupted her reverie.

'Could you get that dear? Priscilla wants to come in.'

I navigated the patches on the carpet, holding my breath as much as possible as I re-entered the flat from the balcony. Miles stood at the door, with an expression of martyrdom on his face. Priscilla trotted in and allowed me to unfasten the leash from her collar. It appeared to be covered in pink spinels, but they may have been rubies.

'You'll have to take off your shoes,' I said.

'But you're wearing the men's slippers. Let me have them.'

'Do you have any poo bags left?'

'Yes, I offloaded the full one.'

'Give me two. I'll put them on my feet.'

He sighed with relief.

'Thanks. These carpets are cesspools of every germ and bacteria known to man. No wonder Noreen is still alive. She's probably immune to death.'

I stifled a guffaw, and we made our way back to the balcony, Priscilla yapping at Miles's feet and biting his trouser legs. He aimed a surreptitious kick at her, but she skipped out of the way with ease. She gave him a savage nip and shook her head from side to side. Miles squeaked.

'Are you okay?' I asked.

He gave Priscilla a glare.

'Oh, don't worry about me, dear. Just a bruised ego. It'll heal.'

'Priscilla adores Miles,' said Noreen, oblivious to the chaos. 'He's her absolute favourite.'

She stared at my feet with disgust. Miles poured himself a cup of Earl Grey and refused a sandwich with a slight grimace.

'Did Priscilla go poo-poo?' asked Noreen.

'Yes, she did. Twice,' said Miles, with emphasis on the word twice.

'Excellent. She had diarrhoea earlier, poor poppet.'

I nearly said I could smell it, but I tried to look concerned instead and turned to face her.

'Um, you said Blackwood was a charlatan. Did you have any reason to think so?'

'I've been rich for most of my life. You can't imagine the number of hangers-on and sycophants I had to put up with during my marriage to Bertie. He had no antenna for that sort of thing. I had to do most of the clearing up. I'm an expert.'

'But didn't you say—'

Miles tried to intervene, but she shushed him.

'I don't remember what I said, but I know what I saw.'

She patted her lap, and Priscilla jumped up and licked her face with the same tongue that had been cleaning her rear end seconds before. I held my breath.

'I saw DI Antrim leaving that day, but there was another person too. I got only a quick glance at them because they left by the service lift.'

'The service lift?' said Miles. 'I didn't know there was a second lift in the building.'

'Yes, it's at the back. People don't use it much because it's prone to breaking down.'

'Did you see a man or a woman?' I asked.

'I don't know. I only got a glance. They were wearing a mackintosh and a fedora to disguise their identity.'

'What time did they leave?'

'I'm not sure. After Antrim. I know that much.'

'And how do you know DI Antrim?'

'He helped me when Bertie died. I don't know what I would have done without him. He's such a dear man.'

She pulled a lace handkerchief out of her sleeve and dabbed at her eyes.

'Did you tell the police about this?' said Miles.

'You tell them. I'm tired.'

'But this is an incredibly important piece of evidence. They'll need to speak to you.'

'Please leave now. Priscilla's tired.'

I glanced at Miles, and he nodded.

'Thank you, Noreen. I'll come and see you again soon. I promise.'

'Don't bring her. I don't like her,' said Noreen, pointing at me.

I tiptoed out of there with poo bags on my feet, picking up my heels on the way. We took the lift downstairs.

'I warned you,' said Miles. 'She can be quite difficult.'

'Money instead of manners. I'll let George know. He can deal with her. I've had enough of dog poo for one investigation.'

Chapter 18

I needed to share Noreen Ashcroft's revelation about the mystery person who used the service lift with George as soon as possible. He had become more tolerant of my interfering in his cases, as he put it, since we had had success solving several murders together. I tried not to antagonise him too much, but relationships with ex-partners are never completely free of needle. I texted him to ask if I could come over and fill him in. He rang me back immediately. George hated typing out long messages.

'Can you come over later after you shut up shop? Somebody died in a house fire last night, and we have to liaise with Brighton after lunch.'

'Sure. Text me when you are free.'

'Just come about five thirty.'

George rang off. Having waved goodbye to Miles, who told me he needed to return home and take a shower, I got down to work at the shop. Mouse had already opened up and bought supplies for the Vintage. We were relatively busy all day, so I didn't have time to dwell on Noreen or her filthy flat.

After we shut up shop, Mouse headed home, and I drove to the police station and parked in the back with the squad cars. The public were not allowed to leave their cars in the police lot, but as the ex-wife of the DI, no one had ever dared challenge me. The young policeman at the gate waved me through with a beam, which I returned.

I entered the station through the back door and passed Flo's laboratory where she carried out most of her forensic testing. She looked up from her work and made signals for tea-drinking. I pointed towards George's office.

'Do you have any news on the case?' she said, popping her head out of the door.

'I think I have a new lead. Well, several actually.'

'Wait for me.'

She grabbed a tablet and came out to greet me with a big hug. As usual, most of her hair had cascaded out of her bun, and she wore a large velvet smock under her white lab coat. She gave me a tight squeeze.

'How's my Mouse?' she said. 'Is he home for the summer?'

'Yes, he's running the Vintage for me. I always get an enormous increase in customer numbers when he's in charge.'

Flo grinned.

'If you've got it, flaunt it,' she said. 'I've got some news too.'

'Why don't you come to supper at the Grotty Hovel on your way home? You can see Mouse and we can eat a takeaway.'

'It's a date.'

We walked through the office, which had old-fashioned glass and metal partitions. Tired doesn't adequately convey the nineteen-eighties vibe it gave out. I felt as if I had walked onto the set of The Bill. George was in his office eating a Kit-Kat which he stuffed in a drawer as I walked in.

'No breakfast,' he said, reddening at being caught.

'I had cake for breakfast,' I said.

He took it back out.

'What are you doing here? Don't tell me Sally buzzed you through without consulting me?'

'It's not her fault. I came in the back way.'

George shook his head.

'They'll let anyone in these days. I must write a memo reminding them we are divorced.'

'And where would I park when I had important leads in your investigation?'

He sighed.

'Let's go to the interview room. I'll get Joe Brennan to join us.'

When we reached the room, I removed my shoes to avoid the electric shocks generated by walking on the nylon carpet. George hated my doing that, but I had once shaken his hand and given him a nasty shock, and after that he didn't complain anymore. The central table had dirty cups and some biscuit crumbs lying on it. I used a tissue to clean my part of the surface. George came in with Joe, and they sat opposite us. I noticed Joe had a grim expression on his face and wouldn't look me in the eye.

'I'm afraid we have terrible news,' said George. 'Before I tell you, I want to assure you that the fault is not yours. It's that awful blogger woman.'

Fear gripped my chest.

'Natalee?' I croaked.

George nodded. A horrible suspicion entered my head.

'She's dead, isn't she?' I said.

'I'm afraid so. We found her remains in the ruins of a house fire. It's strictly confidential for now, but we think it was arson.'

I gasped.

'Arson? Did she die in the fire?' I asked.

'That's what's worrying me. The SOCO told me someone bludgeoned her to death and then set fire to the house to make it look like an accident.'

'She died of head injuries?' I said.

'Yes. We think the murder is related to that of Blackwood, as the method is so similar.'

I shook my head.

'I had planned to tell you about this today, before Raven stole my notes. We spoke to Natalee about Blackwood two days ago. She confirmed our suspicions he was blackmailing people with information he got from their phones. She told us she had planned to leave her husband, and Blackwood found out, so he used that to make her recruit new clients. I got the impression that her husband was violent towards her. She seemed frightened, but she wouldn't leave. She said she had it all under control.'

'I'll check with Brighton and ask them if they have any record of domestic violence at the property,' said George.

'You think it was the same killer?'

'We don't know yet, but you mustn't tell anyone about the cause of death. It's not common knowledge.'

'So, not likely to be a copycat killing then?'

'Who knows? One thing's for sure. It's highly likely her death is related to Blackwood's, and the killer may not be finished yet.'

'What about Raven?' I asked. 'Did she publish her blog yet?'

'About half an hour after she left your shop,' said Joe, 'She mentioned your theories about Natalee Bridges being in danger from her abusive husband.'

An icy chill ran down my spine.

'But we promised Natalee to keep her plan confidential.'

'I doubt her husband saw Raven's blog. It's not exactly popular. Anyway, I tracked her down immediately, and I charged her with endangering an investigation and publishing confidential information. I made her take the blog down. It was only up for about an hour.'

I felt sick.

'Are you sure her husband didn't see it?' I said.

'We are still investigating. Nothing is confirmed yet, but it is not your fault, Tan. Don't go blaming yourself,' said George.

'Did you get my notebook?' I asked.

Joe slapped his forehead.

'Damn! I completely forgot to get it back from her. I promise to make sure she hands it over.'

'Flo tells us you have new leads in the case,' said Joe, taking out his tablet. 'Can you please tell us what you've got?'

I took a deep breath and tried to concentrate. Remembering how Raven had tricked me made me feel sick. I forced myself to speak.

'I spoke to a woman today who lives on the same floor where Vivian Blackwood had his premises. She says someone used the service lift to leave their floor after DI Antrim had gone home the night Blackwood died.'

'Seriously?' said George. 'Not another suspect.'

'What service lift?' said Joe. 'No one told us about a second lift.'

'It's not used every day and is often broken down, according to this lady. I thought you might like to fingerprint it and check the CCTV.'

'Absolutely. We'd like to talk to your witness too,' said Joe. 'What's her name?'

'Noreen Ashcroft. She's a widow and—'

'Bertie's widow! What a coincidence. Doesn't she have that irritating dog? Mr something?' said George.

'He died. She has a bitch now. Priscilla. You'll have to take off your shoes when you enter the flat. Bring some slippers if you want to avoid cholera or septic shock. The flat is putrid with dog wee and poo.'

'That's a relief,' said Flo.

'What is?' said George.

'So far, the circumstantial evidence points to DI Antrim. It seems so out of character for him. Why kill Vivian Blackwood? But now we can look up some other alleyways.'

'I've asked for Blackwood's financials from the bank. DI Antrim told me Blackwood had tried to blackmail him. Obviously, that gives Terry a motive, but he informed me without questioning, so he's being totally transparent. If we can get the names of any clients Blackwood was blackmailing, that will give us a list of prime suspects. We are looking into it right now.'

'Can you tell me about it?'

'No, but ask our son. I'm sure he'll have been beavering away at the cracks in the internet.'

'What's the evidence against DI Antrim?' I asked.

'So far, it's only circumstantial,' said Joe. 'Blackwood's assistant, Titania, told me that Antrim had the last appointment that evening after a regular seance. She let him into the flat and then went on a date at the pub.'

'I suppose you corroborated that statement? She didn't strike me as particularly trustworthy,' I said.

'Why do you say that?' said Flo.

'Oh, I don't know. Instinct.'

'We deal in evidence here, Tan.'

I tried not to roll my eyes and failed. The news about Natalee Hedges had knocked the stuffing out of me.

'Antrim himself admitted to grabbing Blackwood by the lapels. He had motive and opportunity,' said Joe.

'Do you have a murder weapon yet?' I asked.

'The killer bludgeoned Blackwood with a heavy metal bust of some fakir or other. It appears to be unplanned. A spur-of-the-moment loss of control.

Blackwood had no defensive wounds. Someone hit him from behind when he turned his back,' said Flo.

'A crime of passion?' I said.

'Anger rather than love, I'd have thought,' said Flo. 'The skull is almost crushed.'

'What about the people who attended the seance?' I asked. 'Could one of them have stayed behind, perhaps even hidden in the service lift?'

'Possibly. Please don't approach them if you learn something important. Let me know first, so Joe can interview them. Maybe Roz knows some of them? I understand she attended Blackwood's sessions several times.'

'I'll see what I can find out. By the way, I met Craig Latchford at Blackwood's office when we went for the seance. I thought nothing of it at the time, but he's got form. I wondered if he could have anything to do with this.'

'Was he Blackwood's client?' asked George.

'I don't know, but he wanted to see him and Titania wouldn't let him.'

'We'll look into it,' said George. 'Along with the five million other things you've told us.'

'Thanks for coming in,' said Joe. 'Nobody wants to see Terry Antrim go down for this.'

'Please take your car with you,' said George. 'We don't have room for civilian vehicles.'

'Which takeaway would you like?' I asked Flo as we walked back to her office.

'Chinese, please. You choose the dishes, and I'll eat them. I'm sorry about Natalee, but you really had nothing to do with it.'

I gave her a brief hug.

'I can't wait to hear your news. Are you sure you can't give me any clues?'

'Quite sure.'

Chapter 19

I dropped by Mr Chen's on our way home and ordered enough food to feed a battalion. Mr Chen gave us some extra-crispy pancakes with plum filling to eat for dessert. We had been going there for years and earned privileges with him as a result. I scoffed one of them on my way home. It tasted like a little pocket of heaven.

When I got home, Harry had already laid the table and opened a bottle of Rioja. He kissed me hello and brushed the sugar from my chin.

'Have you been sampling the wares?' he said.

Flo had also arrived, and they were sitting on the armchairs debating the merits of various international cuisines. Harry told me Mouse had let out an adorable squeak when he saw Flo and sunk into her ample embrace with a sigh of pleasure. Neither showed any inclination to desist until Harry and I had unpacked the food and set it out on the table. Mouse and Flo extricated themselves from their hug and sat beside each other at the table. We helped ourselves to the delicious food. I wrapped myself a shredded duck pancake and bit into it. The hoisin sauce squirted out of the end all over my fingers. The smell of fried pork balls and battered shrimp filled the room, competing with the sounds of enjoyment emitted by all of us.

Flo finished first. She wiped her mouth with her napkin and sighed with satisfaction.

'I'm so glad you're pursuing these new leads in the Blackwood murder,' she said. 'The Super has been pressuring us to wrap the case up. He's convinced DI Antrim is guilty, despite the lack of a smoking gun.'

'Terry asked me for help,' I said. 'I didn't feel able to refuse.'

'Well, it's not an open and shut case by any means. The fingerprints on the bust of Doris Stokes were smeared beyond recognition. The only anomaly is a set of fingerprints on a teacup in the medium's communication room. I don't have the owner on file. We need to find the people who were at the seance and take theirs for elimination. It's not as easy as you think. Some of Blackwood's clients are unwilling to be identified.'

'If you send me that list, I can check it against the people I saw there. Then Mouse and I will find out why they are not keen on coming forward,' I said.

'Definitely,' said Mouse, rubbing his hands together.

'By the way,' said Flo. 'I have an announcement to make. No one - and that means you, Mouse - is to panic.'

We all turned to listen.

'The Met's cold case team has made an approach to me about working for them. I'm off for an interview next week to talk to them about it.'

'That's amazing,' I said. 'Congratulations.'

'But you can't go,' said Mouse.

'What does Nick think?' asked Harry.

Flo had been going out with Harry's brother Nick since the previous Christmas. We all approved of that development. But they spent much of their time apart, as he lived in Devon.

'I haven't told him yet. There's no point upsetting him until they make me a firm offer.'

'What about upsetting me?' said Mouse, but she ignored him.

'It's a job I've always wanted,' she said 'Anyway, I'm not sure he'd follow me.'

She put her arm around Mouse's shoulders.

'You can come and visit. It's not like London is a million miles away.'

Mouse pouted and refused to be comforted.

'Ignore him,' I said. 'He'll probably work in London himself, with his skills. You can keep an eye on each other.'

After Flo had left, we snuggled on the sofa. Hades kneaded our chests with his paws, rejecting them one by one before jumping down and exiting through the cat flap for a spot of night hunting. I had been forced to put a bell on his collar to slow the massacre of birds and small mammals in the back garden. Since Helen's abortive attempt to clear it, the brambles and nettles had returned with increased vigour. Great for blackberries and hiding bodies, but disappointing for Helen.

'I paid good money for that gardener,' she said, sniffing. 'You could at least have tried to maintain it.'

'But the police cordoned the garden off for weeks after they dug up the body. It really wasn't my fault the brambles took advantage of the lull. Anyway, Hades is ecstatic.'

'And you care what a cat thinks?'

She forgave me after I got her some snowdrop and crocus bulbs to bury in her planters for the following winter.

Harry picked up the remote control.

'Can you face watching the news for a while?' he said. 'I want to see how the Prime Minister is dealing with yet another scandal involving his ministers.'

'They won't tell us,' said Mouse. 'We are plebs. They lie all the time.'

'Because we don't need to know,' I said.

I watched the plump MP defending himself with bluster and prevarication for a while. He reminded me of Craig Latchford, but my eyelids grew heavy, and I dozed off. I dreamt about finding a Faberge egg in a box of junk at a car boot sale. As I reached for my wallet, a sharp nudge caught me in the ribs.

'Oi, you wrecked my dream,' I said. 'I was about to—'

'Cuddle Terry Antrim,' said Harry.

'Don't be silly. He'd stab me in the heart with those bony elbows. I like a bit more body to handle.'

Harry let me squeeze his love handles.

'Okay. Either get a room or watch the local news without flirting,' said Mouse. 'They just announced a woman died in a house fire in the Brighton area. The police are checking for signs of arson.'

'George told me the dead woman was Natalee Hedges,' I said. 'She was also a client of Vivian

Blackwood. Roz and I talked to her on our way home from Brighton when we went to see Zelda Romano.'

'That's terrible,' said Mouse.

'A man is helping the police with their enquiries,' said Harry, still watching the broadcast.

I sighed.

'I hope it's her husband. I'm sure he murdered her, and it may be partially my fault.'

'What do you mean?' said Mouse.

'A blogger stole my notebook yesterday, with all my notes, including some about Natalee. She published a blog that the police took down almost immediately. It included details about Natalee's plans to run away from her home. I'm worried Natalee's husband read it.'

'How is that your fault?' said Harry. 'The blogger should go to prison.'

'She might.'

I tried to smile.

'George would love to lock you up in a cell,' said Harry.

'So would DI Antrim,' said Mouse. 'With him on the inside.'

'That poor man is genuinely helping the police with their enquires and all you two can do is make juvenile remarks. Someone picked up the bust of Doris Stokes and smashed Blackwood's skull in with it. I'm sure it wasn't him.'

'Ah, but do you have any evidence?' said Mouse, imitating George with skill.

'As a matter of fact, I have a new lead. It seems Titania forgot to tell us about the service lift at the back of the building. Noreen Ashcroft says she saw someone use it after Terry left Blackwood's flat.'

'And we've still got to trace that woman from Ghita's step class,' said Mouse. 'I bet the tennis club has a register of the makes of cars owned by its members. I could easily hack their sites and find out who drives a red Fiat Uno.'

'Or you could do it the legal way and chat up the folk at the reception desks of the tennis clubs.'

He pouted again and picked his fingernails. In order to cheer us all up, I told them about Noreen Ashcroft and Priscilla, and how traumatised Miles Quirk became with the whole excrement situation. Once we started laughing, it became impossible to stop.

'He must have been Wee-lly horrified,' said Harry.

'Did Noreen have a cock-a-poo?' said Mouse.

'I think it was a spread-a-poo,' I replied.

And so on. It's amazing how a little toilet humour can cheer up the British people. We are infantile when it comes to bodily functions. When we had stopped giggling, I grabbed a new A5 notebook to make notes about my meeting at the station and Flo's comments about the case.

'Uh oh, Poirot has made an appearance,' said Harry. 'It can't be long before the suspects are gathered together in the drawing room for the grim recap of the murder and the naming of the killer.'

I sighed.

'I don't feel like solving this murder. I miss my old notebook. Joe forgot to get it back from Raven Huxley. Will I ever see it again?'

'Joe will find her. She can't have gone far. Anyway, DI Antrim needs you to prove someone else murdered Blackwood. You can't give up just because someone stole your notebook.'

'I don't think we're anywhere close to exonerating Terry Antrim yet. You heard what Flo said. He's still the prime suspect.'

'He trusts you for a reason,' said Harry. 'Carry on regardless, as you always do. The truth will out eventually.'

But did I even want to know the truth?

Chapter 20

The next morning, Mouse and I met Roz at Second Home. She had been out to sea with Ed, and she had a sparkle in her eye that had been missing since her mother died. It made me happy to know she was dealing better with her loss. We had coffee upstairs while I updated her on the case. I was always careful with the information I shared, but I felt she had a right to know more about Blackwood and his nefarious schemes.

'I went to see a nutty woman with Miles Quirk yesterday. She lived in the same building and on the same floor as Vivian Blackwood.'

Roz's eyes opened wide.

'You mean Noreen Ashcroft and her Pomeranian from hell, Priscilla Poo-paws?'

'The very one. I should've realised you'd know who she is.'

'I'm still the queen of gossip in this town. I could tell you tales about her ex-husband's exploits that would shrivel your kidneys.'

'Please don't.'

'Honestly, can we change the subject?' said Mouse. 'I'm trying to eat.'

We still needed to find out how Blackwood had been spying on his clients' private information. I felt as if this could be the key to finding the murderer. While Mouse had his doubts about the use of any kind of spyware to garner the information, I wanted to eliminate the possibility before we moved forward in the investigation. As I knew she would, Roz handed over her mobile phone as soon as Mouse asked for it. It didn't take long for him to establish the absence of software apps necessary for spying.

'What about your mother's phone?' said Mouse.

'It's in a drawer in my house, but I never took it anywhere near Blackwood's flat,' said Roz.

'Perhaps I disturbed Titania before she had time to install the software,' I said.

'So how did Blackwood get my private information?' asked Roz.

'It's a mystery, for now. We needed someone else's phone to check it for signs of interference. Was there anyone at the seance you trusted?'

Roz scratched her head.

'Emily. We could try asking her. It depends on what she believes after all the publicity in the Herald. The last article practically called Blackwood a con man, but it didn't offer any proof. Let me talk to her. Maybe I can persuade her to let you examine her phone.'

'That would be great. We really need to speak to Titania as well. She must know more than she's saying. It's inconceivable Blackwood could run any scheme without her knowledge.'

'I doubt she'd talk to you,' said Mouse. 'If you found her untrustworthy, it's likely she noticed. You're not good at hiding your true feelings.'

'She certainly isn't,' said Roz, laughing. 'She can't lie to save her life.'

'Yes, I can. Well, no, maybe not. Can you find out what Titania's into? Maybe we can throw you across her path?'

'I don't like the sound of that,' said Mouse. 'But I'll have a go.'

'And I'll speak to Emily,' said Roz. 'I'll cycle round to her house.'

'Why don't you take her some of Ghita's shortbread? No one can resist that sort of temptation.'

While Mouse delved into Titania's internet history and Roz cycled off to ambush Emily with some shortbread, I got to work on the accounts. Mouse had set up accounting software on my tablet, but I still used the paper ledger at the shop. I planned to transfer the information at some stage before the end of the tax year, a task I was dreading. When I had finished recording the transactions in the ledger, I glanced up at the street windows of Second Home and noticed how filthy they looked. The seagulls had done their usual trick of spraying the glass with liquid faeces, like flying Priscillas. The memory of Noreen's putrid flat made me feel quite faint. Even cleaning seagull poo was preferable to another visit there.

I removed the cleaning equipment from the back cupboard and filled a bucket with warm, soapy water. Then I fastened my apron and staggered outside with the heavy bucket. The warm day soon made the task more enjoyable, and I sang as I scrubbed at the windowpanes.

'You should join a choir,' said Mouse, appearing at the door of the shop. 'You've got a fantastic voice.'

'I used to. I sang with a band, you know.'

His eyes widened.

'No, really? Are you pulling my leg?'

'The Red Herrings,' said Roz, arriving back to the shop on her bicycle. 'She was our lead singer.'

'How come I don't know about this?' said Mouse.

'I don't tell you everything. Anyway, you never asked.'

'Can I see you on the internet?'

'I shouldn't think so. This was back in the Stone Age, before computers.'

'You're not that old.'

'The internet was too slow for that sort of shenanigan,' said Roz. 'We were strictly a live band.'

'We made a tape though, remember?' I said. 'Whatever happened to it?'

'It's probably still in my mother's attic in a cardboard box. She thought we were crap.'

'No, she didn't. Not if she'd kept the cassette all these years.'

'She might have thrown it away.'

'Or not,' said Mouse. 'I'd pay a lot to hear it.'

'I've got to clear the attic out sometime,' said Roz. 'If you clear it for me, you can have the tape.'

'I'm not sure I like the sound of that. It's my recording too.'

Mouse made sad kitten eyes at me. He learned it from Hades.

'Please.'

I sighed heavily.

'Okay, but only you can listen to it.'

I should have noticed his lack of reply to this order, but a speeding car almost knocked over my bucket and distracted me.

'What did Emily say?'

'She didn't seem keen. I think most people are embarrassed by their association with Blackwood now they know he was a fraud.'

'I think Harry had it right,' said Mouse. 'Blackwood may not have been clairvoyant, but he still helped people get over their losses.'

'Didn't you tell George that Blackwood had a blackmail racket going?'

'That's the rumour online. But do we have any proof yet?'

'Maybe we can get George to update us? I'll call him and ask him when he will have time.'

To my surprise, George came straight over. He demanded a glass of water and asked us all upstairs for a debrief. I locked the shop door and turned the sign to closed. We trooped upstairs, and I gave George his water. He sank into his chair with relief.

'I thought you should know,' he said, gulping down the whole glass in one go. 'We've found some of Blackwood's accounts and nearly everyone who attended the seance, present company excepted, had deposited sizeable sums of money into his bank account. They are all prime suspects, along with DI Antrim.' He wiped his mouth with his sleeve. 'You may be in danger, Roz, so I recommend you spend your nights out at sea with that husband of yours until we figure out what's going on.'

'Okay,' said Roz. 'We'll have to postpone the cassette hunt for another time.'

'Cassette?' said George. 'What's that got to do with the murder? This isn't Columbo, you know.'

'Nothing, Dad. We were talking about the Red Herrings earlier, and Roz said she might still have a tape of them performing, stored in a box in the attic.'

George stared at me, and then through me, his memories reviving.

'I fell in love with you when I first saw you singing in the band, Tan,' he said. 'I'll never forget it.'

I swallowed, lost for words. I thought Roz might faint with surprise at this unexpected revelation. Mouse recovered first.

'I play the electric guitar, you know,' he said. 'I'm pretty good, even though I say so myself.'

'I've heard you play. You're not that good,' said George.

'Rohan told me Ghita still plays the drums on her saucepans when one of her favourite songs comes on the radio,' said Roz. 'She's not forgotten how.'

I laughed.

'You're all crackers. We were terrible.'

George patted my hand to attract my attention.

'The bad old days weren't that awful, were they?' he said.

An enormous lump formed in my throat.

'No. We were young, and we had a lot of fun,' I said, standing up to break the spell.

I almost expected to be wearing platform heels.

'Nostalgia,' said Roz, 'Is not what it used to be.'

Chapter 21

It didn't take the local papers long to find the link between Natalee Hedges and Vivian Blackwood. A rash of conspiracy theories appeared online, each more ridiculous than the last. One anonymous poster suggested Natalee had been murdered by Vivian's ghost in revenge for her killing him first. George was beside himself with annoyance and refused to share any details of the case with me, despite my swearing I had nothing to do with any of it.

'Why is your pal Jim Swift at the Seacastle Herald spreading false rumours?' he asked. 'Who fed him the information? That's what I'd like to know.'

I ignored him. The case was getting to him. He would calm down.

Initially, Titania Grafton, Blackwood's assistant, had refused to come to Second Home or to speak to me at all about the goings-on at his headquarters. I didn't have any way of forcing her to speak to me, but I felt as if she might hold the key to the murder. Mouse suspected her of spreading some of the rumours going around about the murderer. It crossed my mind she might even be responsible. Mouse got onto his tablet and soon found the flaw in her defences. Perhaps unsurprisingly, Titania belonged to a hacker club called Mouse's Minions.

'The clue's in the name, Mum. I'm her role model,' he said, puffing up his chest.

I never understood quite what he had done to earn his fame, and I had long ago let bygones be bygones, especially as he now used his skills in a forensic computing degree instead. He asked Titania to come to the Vintage, but she refused several times. I had almost given up, but then the news that Natalee Hedges had not died in the fire but had been murdered emerged, and suddenly Titania changed her tune. It turned out we were not the only people who thought Titania had something to do with Blackwood's schemes, and she wondered if she might be next.

By the time she turned up dressed in full Goth regalia with every piercing occupied, she had worked herself into a complete meltdown. She glanced outside at the street, fear oozing from her pores.

'Lock the door,' she said. 'They're after me.'

'You'll be safe upstairs,' I said. 'I promise not to let anyone in.'

She ran up the stairs to the Vintage, tripping on one because she kept looking back at the entrance. Mouse took her to the window table.

'You can watch the street from here,' he said. 'You're perfectly safe.'

I put the latch on the door and came upstairs. The look of panic on her face was almost comical.

'They killed her,' she said. 'They killed Natalee for helping him. She didn't mean any harm. She couldn't pay him you see.'

'Surely she could stop going if she couldn't afford to see Blackwood,' said Mouse.

Titania shook her head. 'You don't understand. He knew things about his clients. He made them pay him to keep their secrets.'

'What did he know about Natalee?' I asked.

'Vivian found out she was planning to leave her abusive husband. He threatened to tell him. When she begged him not to, he asked her for money.'

'Why would Natalee be talking about her affair to a medium? Did he hypnotise her to extract her secrets?'

Titania laughed.

'He couldn't hypnotise a goldfish. We used technology.'

She clamped her hand over her mouth. Mouse shook his head and smiled at her.

'That's rad,' he said with fake admiration. 'You can't keep it a secret from me. You've got to tell me how you did it.'

'I can't.'

'It will all come out eventually, but if you don't tell us, we can't keep you safe.'

I looked out of the window and pretended to do a double take. She gasped.

'Is someone out there?'

'A person in a raincoat and a fedora. I thought they might be casing the place, but maybe they were looking at the lamps in the window…'

Titania had gone white as a sheet.

'Noreen told me the man who murdered Vivian escaped in the lift dressed like that.'

'Did she? That's what she told me too. Can you think of anyone who wears a hat to your office?'

'No, I've no idea who it was. It might have been Craig Latchford, though. He had it in for Vivian.'

'Why do you say that?'

'They had a project together, which went wrong. Vivian knew something about Craig that he held over him. Craig had threatened to hurt him if he didn't leave him alone.'

'You need to tell us how Vivian learned about these private matters. It may be the only way we can find the killer and stop him or her coming to look for you.'

'It would be simpler to show you.'

Mouse nodded vigorously at me.

'I think I can get permission for us to enter the flat,' I replied. 'Give me a minute.'

I went downstairs and called the police station. Joe Brennan agreed to come over immediately and take us to Blackwood's flat. He gathered a team of forensic officers to accompany him, and soon he tooted his horn outside the shop. Titania jumped about two feet in the air, and I had to swallow a guffaw.

'You said nothing about police,' she said.

'You didn't ask,' I said, directing her downstairs. 'Serves her right,' I whispered to Mouse.

We locked the shop and got into the patrol vehicle. Behind us, another vehicle contained the SOCO crew's electronic experts. Mouse rubbed his hands together.

'My first proper case,' he said. 'I can't wait.'

We pulled up at Vivian Blackwood's building and rode up in the lift. I noticed Titania leaning towards Mouse, but he moved right to the side, so he wasn't in contact with her. She tried to bite her nails, but they were too short and looked raw already. I pretended I hadn't noticed.

When we arrived at Blackwood's floor, Joe took shoe covers, paper jumpsuits, and hairnets out of the bag he carried.

'I know you two have been here already, but I don't want SOCO further confused,' he said.

He spoke to the officer in charge of the forensic team, and they waited as we struggled into the suits, and I stuffed my hair into a net. Mouse bit his lip to keep a laugh in when he saw me.

'I think the Smurfs may have competition,' he said. 'Hilarious.'

'Everybody ready? Let's go,' said Joe, taking out a key.

He opened the door of the flat and we filed in. Titania had a sulky look on her face and trailed in last. I guess she had second thoughts about revealing their methods in front of a police officer, but she had realised too late how it might look to him - Look, officer. This is how we blackmailed our clients.

'Miss Grafton? It's your turn to shine,' said Joe, waving her forward. 'How did Blackwood read his client's minds, or their diaries?'

Titania sighed. 'It's not rocket science. We used hidden cameras. There's one up there and another and one hidden in the plasterwork. When clients waited outside, they almost always took out their phones. Scrolling their lives away, as you do.'

'I don't,' I said, even though I spent far too much time doing exactly that.

'What were the cameras for?' said Joe.

'Recording the passwords. When people went into the inner vestibule to consult with Vivian, I reviewed the footage on the computer and wrote down their passwords.'

'That's why you wanted us to leave our mobile phones with you,' I said.

'Correct. When first-time clients went inside to see Vivian, he'd take his time with them. He'd gently coax basic information out of them while waiting for me to get into their mobiles. I only needed a minute or two to enter their passwords and to scroll through their messages searching for material he could use. You'd be amazed what people reveal to their family and close friends on their phones. I'd transcribe it onto their file, or if it was relevant, I'd tell Vivian on his earpiece so he could reveal his conversations with the deceased and amaze the clients.'

'And the blackmail?'

'Sometimes I'd find some juicy gossip or references to dodgy dealings on the phone. Then I'd copy it down and give it to Vivian after the client had gone home. He used that information to suggest people might like to donate to his business.'

Joe reached into his pocket and took out a piece of paper with photographs of people on it. I spotted Roz and DI Antrim among them.

'Can you tell me by what names you knew these people?' he asked.

Titania went through the people one by one. I noticed Mouse's fingers flying over the keyboard of his mobile phone. Good lad.

'And what about you, Miss Grafton? How did you benefit from this activity?' said Joe.

'I didn't. Vivian knew things about me too. He threatened to reveal my secrets if I didn't help him.'

'I don't think that's going to wash with my boss,' said Joe. 'I'll need you to come down to the station with me and make a statement. But first, you need to help the SOCOs to locate all the surveillance equipment.'

'But I haven't done anything wrong.'

'Then you don't need to worry.'

'You'll be as safe as houses at the jail. Nobody can attack you there,' I said.

'Who would attack her?' said Joe. 'I think you two had better go. Thanks Tanya.'

'Can't I stay?' said Mouse.

'You're not on the force yet,' said Joe. 'Thanks for coming.'

'But you promised to help me,' said Titania.

'We have,' I replied.

Chapter 22

We left Titania standing like a small white monument in the centre of Blackwood's flat, surrounded by SOCOs in blue coveralls ripping wiring out of walls. Joe had his tablet out and typed copious notes onto it. He seemed to have forgotten us in an instant.

As we removed our suits and shoe covers, Mouse sulked.

'How will we get home?' he said.

'We'll walk,' I said. 'It's not far.'

'Not for you. I'll call an Uber.'

'I'm walking, and so are you. It's a lovely day out there, and I need to clear my head.'

'Whatever.'

The lift clanked and groaned on its way down.

'I hate creaky lifts,' said Mouse. 'I always think I'm about to get stranded.'

'I doubt it's serious,' I said. 'Most lifts seem to spend their lives complaining, a bit like Marvin the Paranoid Android.'

'Marvin the who?'

'Ancient history. Never mind.'

We stepped out into bright sunshine, and I took a couple of deep breaths.

'Do you think Titania is caught up in Blackwood's schemes?' said Mouse.

'I think she's clever enough. And we only have her word for it about leaving before Antrim. She could easily have waited for him to go home and killed Blackwood herself. Flo told us he had no defensive wounds, so he felt safe with whoever murdered him,' I said.

'Dad will find out. He won't be fooled by her defenceless girl act.'

'You realise this discovery makes everyone a suspect.'

'Only until the techy guys finish checking Blackwood's bank accounts. Anyone who paid more than the price of an appointment will be added to the suspect list.'

The prevailing wind blew straight at us as we walked back into town. I regretted my refusal of a taxi as it penetrated my thin top and blew my hair into a bird's nest. As we neared a bench on the promenade, I noticed a plump woman hunched over her knees. Her shoulders were shaking, and I realised she was sobbing her heart out. Not being one to mind my own business, I stopped in front of her and touched her gently on the arm. She looked up at us, her eyes wild.

'Are you okay?' I said, and then I recognised her. 'Aren't you Emily Carradine? My friend Roz knows you.'

'Who are you?' she said.

'I'm Tanya Bowe.'

She wailed.

'I knew it. The police have sent you to arrest me, haven't they? They think I murdered Natalee.'

I don't know who was more startled by this statement, Mouse or me.

'Um, what makes you think that?'

'It's all my fault. I shouldn't have sent him the letter, but he deserved it. I'm surprised he lasted so long. Everybody had it in for him.'

I had no idea what she was talking about, but if she wanted to talk, I wanted to listen.

'We're going back to my café. Would you like to come and have a cup of coffee and a slice of cake? You look as if you could do with a sugar rush.'

She gave us a brief smile.

'Is it far?'

'I'll call an Uber,' said Mouse, and he caught my eye.

'Go ahead,' I said. 'I'll pay.'

It took only five minutes to drive to the shop. Emily went straight upstairs and sat in a comfy armchair, still snivelling into a now sodden tissue. I offered her a new one.

'Now then, what would you like to drink?'

'I'll have a pot of tea please, and what's that cake? It looks like a Battenburg?'

'Ah, it's our friend Ghita's latest invention, a Citrus Battenburg. Would you like to try it?'

'Yes, please. I really need that sugar rush you offered me. I feel quite faint.'

I interpreted this as asking for a large piece of cake, and she did not complain when I placed a thick slab in front of her. She ate it with a fork and did not leave a single crumb on her plate. She drank two cups of tea, gulping them down as if she hadn't drunk for a week. Then she daintily patted her lips.

'Thank you. I can feel the sugar entering my veins like a shot of heroin.'

'I'm glad it helps. Could you please explain why you went to see Natalee Hedges last week?'

'She's the one who recommended Blackwood to me. I asked her whether she knew about the blackmail. She laughed at me and sent me away. I thought she might help me, you know, join up with me to fight evil. But I guess I watch too many Marvel movies.'

'You know the police think somebody murdered her before setting the house on fire?'

She avoided my inquisitive glance.

'I heard. But it wasn't me. I couldn't kill a fly, honest.'

'You said you sent a letter. To whom?'

'Blackwood, of course. I threatened to expose him as a fraud if he didn't stop blackmailing his clients. Haven't the police found it yet?'

'I'm afraid I'm not privy to that information.'

'My fingerprints will be all over it. I'm not much of a criminal, am I?'

'I shouldn't worry,' I said. 'You're not at the top of the suspect list yet. Can you tell me why you went to see Blackwood in the first place?'

She raised her head and stared at Mouse.

'It's private. I don't think I could talk about it in front of a man.'

'Oh, don't worry about me, dear. I'm as gay as an Easter Bonnet,' said Mouse.

I raised an eyebrow at him, but he ignored me. Emily rearranged her layered skirts.

'Oh well, I suppose it will all come out in the investigation. I lost a baby more than a decade ago. I was six months pregnant by then, and I had formed a strong attachment to her.'

She blew her nose loudly into her tissue. An old pain awoke in my chest and twisted like a knife. I tried to ignore it and force it back into hiding.

'I'm so sorry. What a dreadful blow!'

'Yes, um, well, when I started to miscarry, they told me to come into the hospital. I didn't realise there was no hope for the baby. I thought they might put it in an incubator, but it didn't survive. A nurse came to see me afterwards and told me the truth. She said I'd get over it and I was lucky I wouldn't be a single mother after all. Everybody agreed it was the best thing for me. I asked to see my baby, but she told me it had gone to the incinerator.'

Mouse gasped.

'But what about bereavement counselling? Couldn't you complain?'

Emily shook her head at him.

'In those days, a miscarriage was treated like a headache or a minor inconvenience. The mother and father's grief was not taken seriously. I was left to get over it by myself. Anyway, the pain of losing my baby got worse over the years instead of better.'

'What did you do?' asked Mouse.

'I mourned for her. I thought I'd never get over it, but then I met Natalee Hedges, and she recommended I see Vivian Blackwood. She told me that if I could communicate with my baby, I might feel better.'

'And you leapt at the chance?' I said.

'Not exactly, but I was desperate. You can't imagine the suffering I endured.'

Actually, I could. All too well. But I made a sympathetic noise.

'So I went to see Vivian, and he helped me work through the grief. He was amazing. I started thinking I could recover.'

She blew her nose again, and her bottom lip wobbled.

'But somehow he found out about the baby's father, and then he turned nasty. He threatened to tell the school where I worked about my pregnancy. He said they'd fire me for breaching safeguarding protocols, even though it was years ago and they don't cover the children's parents. I could lose my job. I'm single. If I don't work, I don't eat.'

'Why didn't you go to the police?'

'Shame mostly, and I felt responsible. If I hadn't had an affair with a parent, none of this would have happened. It's ruined my life. I hated Blackwood. When I heard someone had murdered him, I danced around the flat.'

Emily's revelations had overwhelmed me. I couldn't react. Mouse noticed my distress and took over the interview.

'You need to go straight to the police and make a statement. Tell them the truth. They'll have to check your story, but everything will be alright.'

'But the baby's father...'

'I very much doubt the police will be interested at this stage. Your testimony that Blackwood blackmailed you will be vital to the case.'

She wiped her eyes and attempted a smile.

'Do you think so? Whoever killed him did the world a favour. I wouldn't tell the police even if I knew who did it.'

'Definitely,' said Mouse. 'Can you get home from here or will I call you an Uber?'

'I'll take the bus to the supermarket, thanks. Don't worry about me. I feel better already.'

Mouse showed her out and then came back upstairs with a look of concern on his face.

'You've gone silent,' he said. 'Are you okay?'

'Just tired,' I said. 'Let's get out of here.'

I could tell he didn't believe me, but I didn't feel able to give him the reason. When we got back to the Grotty Hovel, I went straight upstairs and lay curled up on our bed. Hades jumped up beside me and pushed his face into mine. I choked on a sob and pulled him close, sniffing his fur. For once, he didn't object and let me draw comfort from him. Not long afterwards, Harry came in and sat on the edge of the bed.

'Are you okay, sweetheart?' he said, stroking my hair. 'Mouse is worried about you.'

I intended to lie, but my excuse caught in my throat, and I couldn't answer.

Harry pulled me to a sitting position and looked deep into my eyes.

'I can see the pain,' he said. 'What the hell's going on? Mouse told me about Emily. Honestly, I would have killed Blackwood myself if I'd known what he was up to, but I don't understand why you are so upset. I thought you didn't know this woman.'

'I didn't. It's not about her. It's about me. There's something I haven't told you. The only person who knows is George, but he blocked it out. He's not much good at tragedy.'

I tried to smile, but tears ran down my cheeks like rivers of lava burning my soul.

'You must tell me,' said Harry. 'This is no time for secrets.'

I sighed.

'Okay, but don't interrupt me while I tell you.'

Chapter 23

George had not been happy when I fell pregnant during our marriage. Having produced a son, Mouse, with his first wife, he had lost interest in procreation and made it clear to me. When I told him about the (unplanned) pregnancy, he muttered things like 'don't expect me to help, I'm far too busy for child-minding and so on'. His attitude had disappointed me, but my instincts told me he would soon mellow when his child appeared. It never occurred to me I would not have a full-term pregnancy. None of my friends had miscarried babies as far as I knew, and although nervous about giving birth I didn't expect any major hiccups.

The pregnancy was not smooth sailing. I had terrible morning sickness, and my feet swelled like plump piglets, making it hard to wear shoes and impossible to squeeze into my pixie boots. I developed several food aversions and found cooking smells an ordeal. Then, in my fourth month, terrible cramps racked my abdomen, and I drove myself to A&E. The nurse who admitted me was old-school and informed me with the minimum of fuss that I might lose my baby. I begged them to save it, but my body had spontaneously rejected it because of a genetic defect.

'There is no heartbeat,' she said, holding the stethoscope against my stomach. 'It's dead. I'm sorry, but the sooner we get rid of it, the safer it will be for you.'

'Her,' I said. 'She's a girl.'

She ignored me and bustled off to book the theatre.

Frantic, I had tried to call George, but he wasn't in the office. Then I remembered he had gone to Brighton to interview a suspect. He ignored his mobile phone and turned it off during interrogations only to be reminded to turn it back on again by exasperated colleagues. Roz had gone fishing with Ed, and Ghita didn't answer her phone either. I wanted to send messages pleading for help, but I couldn't think what to write. 'Come quick, I'm losing my baby' seemed over dramatic. The nurse decided for me.

'You're very lucky. Both a theatre and a surgeon are available immediately. We can't delay. Leave your husband's number with me and I'll get hold of him. You must go to surgery now.'

When I woke later, woozy and disoriented, I found myself in a maternity ward with all the associated sounds and sights. I saw a tiny baby in a cot between my bed and the next. For a moment, I believed my baby had survived, but the woman next door reached over and stroked its tummy. I covered my head with a sheet as the reality hit me. I couldn't upset the other mothers. I had to get out of there immediately before someone said something unfortunate to me and the dam broke. Then, George appeared at the end of my bed, looking grave.

'You're all right,' he said. 'I thought it was an emergency.'

'I lost the baby,' I said. 'It feels like an emergency to me.'

His face worked as he fought to find the right thing to say. I almost felt sorry for him.

'Please take me home,' I said. 'I can't stand another minute in this place.'

Relief flooded his features, and I knew he had seized on my plea as an actionable task. I hadn't realised until then how married to the job he had become and how little my worries mattered to him. He never mentioned it, but he had dreaded being forced into the parental role again. Never was a man less suited to owning an emotion. He didn't mean to be cruel, but he had always seen the world through his own lens. I'd like to think he has changed now that he's older and less driven. Then, I joined him in a conspiracy of silence and pretended to get over it and return to normal, as he fervently wished.

After I had recovered physically, I fell into a deep clinical depression from which I could not emerge. George, being of the opinion that depression was a form of malingering, tolerated me at first, but soon became impatient at my lack of progress. I don't remember if he actually suggested I pull my socks up, but he insinuated it, despite being assured by our GP that clinical depression was a genuine and common result of losing a baby. George found it incomprehensible and couldn't understand what had happened to his happy wife. He came home from work later and later, and that's when Sharon happened.

Harry had not interrupted once during my story. He had nodded and frowned and looked stricken at times, but he had respected my right to tell the story without killing the flow. He stroked my hair.

'Why didn't you tell me?' he asked. 'That day in the van on the way to the manor at Little Stebbing, with the cows and the mud?'

My memory gave me a clear flashback of the scene. Harry had asked me if I wanted children, and I had lied and said, not really. He had told me his wife, Cathy, had tried for years before dying of ovarian cancer.

'I don't know. We weren't a couple at that stage. I guess I didn't want to tell you something so private.'

I thought he might cry. He wrapped his arms around me and buried his face in my hair for a short while. Then he lifted his head and looked me directly in the eye.

'Could you still have a baby? If you wanted one, I mean. Could we?'

I blinked away tears as I struggled with his question.

'Um, I don't know. Maybe. I'm a little old now. Forty-one is not the first flush of youth.'

He shrugged.

'Now's not the time to discuss this, us, but if you still want a baby, I'm game.'

I looked at him in astonishment.

'Seriously?'

'One hundred per cent.'

'Can we talk about this another day, when the time is right?'

'Of course, but don't wait too long. Mouse isn't getting any younger, and we need him to babysit.'

We revelled in a warm embrace as time stood still for a moment. Then, the door creaked and fell open. Mouse stood startled on the threshold.

'I'm sorry. I shouldn't have been listening, but I was so worried about you, Mum.'

'Too late,' said Harry. 'Act now, apologise later.'

'That's okay, darling. I would have told you everything anyway. Come here and have a cuddle. You're my only baby for now, and I'm taking advantage before I lose you to another woman.'

Chapter 24

The next morning, I woke feeling different about everything. It's hard to describe my lightness of spirit. I gazed at Harry as he slept, his arm flung out along the pillow. My heart filled with love and panic in equal measure. Could I really take the leap into motherhood at this stage in life? Would I regret it if I didn't? I took a brief shower and got dressed to go to the shop.

Hades came upstairs demanding his breakfast, and I shooed him back downstairs. His raised tail spoke of his triumph as I followed him into the kitchen and dug out a sachet of salmon in jelly. I tore open the sachet and expelled the contents into his bowl. He stuck his face into the food and gobbled it as if he hadn't been fed for a week. I sneaked a look at the fridge door and reviewed the sticker with the date of his last worming tablet. Damn! Luckily, Mouse would volunteer to make Hades take one, as the last time I tried to make Hades swallow a tablet he inflicted a nasty bite on my index finger. He finished his breakfast and looked up at me, licking his lips expectantly. He tried a tentative meow, but I shook my head.

'Not today, worm boy. No more breakfast.'

I wrote a note to Mouse asking him to give Hades his worming tablet, which I left on the kitchen table. I added a smiley face. He would sigh and make a fuss, but he liked the fact Hades trusted him sufficiently to allow him to administer the medicine. I fancied a chocolate croissant for breakfast, so I set out for my appointment at the hairdresser without eating.

A trip to the hairdresser can be therapeutic if your stylist is a genius and makes you look like a film star. Marge Dawson could create a Parisian-level coiffure from a bird's nest while soothing you with gossip from all corners of Seacastle. She always asked me if I was going somewhere nice first, to dispense with formalities before launching into the latest scandal warming people's ears and keyboards. I had never introduced her to Roz on the grounds professional jealousy might cause a catfight, but she would have been stiff competition. I always booked my appointment weeks ahead to let the anticipation build. She wasn't cheap, but I always walked out of there feeling like a million dollars.

When I flopped into her chair after having my hair washed, she tutted at me and shook her head. In truth, I wasn't looking my best, but her idea of glamour was her hand-knitted cardigans in clashing yarns with dropped stitches, which I always complimented to the skies. Being kind is free and unlocks unexpected doors.

'Thanks, dearie,' she said. 'Going anywhere nice this year?'

'No, but I'm hoping to help send someone to the nick,' I said, winking at her in the mirror.

'Another case?' She put up her hand to stall my reply. 'Wait, let me guess. Oh! It's that awful man, isn't it? That psychic or whatever he called himself. A blaggard from what I hear. He got what was coming to him.'

'And what did you hear?' I asked, trying to keep my voice neutral. 'You should join the police.'

'I tried. They won't have me. I'm too old and I can't use their computers.'

'They don't know what they're missing. Huggy Bear had nothing on you.'

She smirked.

'And which is your ex? Starsky or Hutch?'

'I think Kojak is closer.'

We had a fit of giggles, egging each other on with facial expressions and pretend lollipops. When we calmed down, she pursed her lips.

'I heard something that might be useful. About those sisters.'

'Which sisters?'

'The Huxleys. I heard Raven stole your notebook. She's been bragging about it all over town. She had no right.'

I froze.

'Raven? Do you know where to find her? The police are flummoxed.'

'Unfortunately, I don't, but I heard she's preparing a blog about Blackwood and Craig Latchford next. She'll expose—'

I spun my chair around to face her.

'Where did you hear this? It's vital we find her. One person may already have died because of her carelessness.'

Marge's eyes opened wide, and she stepped backwards.

'Died? Oh my goodness, you mean Natalee Hedges, don't you? I hadn't put two and two together.'

'Listen, Marge. It's really important that you don't mention this to anyone. Lives are in danger, and you can save them, but you have to keep quiet from now on.'

She sat down in the swivel chair beside me.

'Was it the same murderer?'

'The police don't know yet, but they're sure Raven's blog precipitated Natalee's murder one way or another. We have to stop Raven from publishing any more of my theories from my notebook before someone gets hurt.'

Marge sighed.

'I promised I wouldn't tell anyone about the blog.'

'Whoever told you doesn't have to know I spoke to you. The police can pretend they got a tip-off.'

'Don't get me wrong. I've no idea where Raven is, and I certainly don't hold with her stealing from you. The person who told me about her is Titania Grafton. She used to work for Blackwood before he, before they, well you know.'

'Titania? We've met. In Blackwood's office.'

'You're not another one of his victims I hope.'

'No, I'm not a fan of clairvoyance. I prefer to let sleeping dogs lie.'

'Dead dogs,' said Marge. 'Do you want me to use hair spray?'

I rang George as soon as I emerged from the hairdresser's, my wallet lighter after giving Marge a huge tip. I suppose she qualified as an informant, but I couldn't imagine how I would charge that to the expenses in my tax bill.

'Titania Grafton? She disappeared after helping Joe find the CCTV circuits in Blackwood's flat. We're having serious trouble breaking into the office computer. The techy blokes say it's protected by massive firewalls and other stuff I don't understand,' said George.

'Oh, that makes sense.'

'What does?'

'She belongs to a group of hackers called Mouse's Minions. They are fans of your son, apparently. Not that he does that anymore.'

'Not that he'd tell you if he did.'

I considered this. Mouse spent his whole life on his laptop. I found it highly likely that his degree course had enhanced rather than diminished his skills in that department.

'Why don't you offer him some consultancy? I can't pay him much for his help in the Vintage. He could really do with the money, and Titania has a crush on him, so I suspect he could persuade her to share a password or two. If she cooperates, can you offer her immunity from prosecution?'

'That very much depends on what she has done. She's not out of the frame for killing Blackwood yet, and we suspect she may have tried to divert funds from Blackwood's accounts into her own.'

'And she seemed so nice,' I said, insincerely.

'She's a vicious little cow.'

'That's not how I would put it, but now you mention it, yes. Will I ask Mouse to head for the station? Roz can mind the fort.'

'Do we have any choice?'

173

Chapter 25

I put my phone into my handbag and headed down the High Street, intending to buy something tasty at Greggs for my and Roz's lunch. Before I had gone fifty yards down the road, my phone rang. I dug it out expecting it to be George again, but Terry Antrim's name appeared on the screen.

'Miz Bowe. It's me. DI Antrim. I was wondering if you wanted to meet for a sandwich and a catch-up at the Ocean Café?'

'Right now?'

'There's no time like the present.'

'Give me fifteen minutes. I need to buy lunch for Roz at the shop.'

'Take your time. I'll be in the Mezzanine.'

I texted Roz and asked her what she wanted from Greggs and then hustled my way down the full pavement to Second Home. Roz wanted to come with me to meet Antrim, but I promised to tell her everything I had learnt from Marge and anything I would learn from him when I got back. Despite Terry Antrim telling me to take my time, I couldn't help hurrying towards the pier and down the boardwalk to the café. The Ocean sat at the sea end of the pier and poked out into the waves like a stranded ship. I pushed my way through the swing doors and entered the bustling restaurant with its symphony of cutlery clinking on china plates and the occasional roar of laughter. A murmur of gossip and chat surrounded me as I ascended to the Mezzanine past the gorgeous fish-life wallpaper in the stairwell.

I spotted Terry immediately. He had arranged his limbs on a window seat shaped like a seashell and resembled a spider crab who had devoured a scallop and now reclined in its empty covering. He smiled at me as I approached, but he looked as if he hadn't slept in days. He hadn't shaved either. It shook me to see him so downcast. He gave me a peck on the cheek, and I waited for him to speak. I noticed he had a pen in his hand, which he twirled incessantly, his thin fingers worrying it round and round.

'You look nice. Have you had your hair done?' he said, glancing up at me from under his lashes. 'Harry is a lucky man. If I had seen you first…'

'George saw me first.'

He laughed.

'I had forgotten about George. He would not have been keen on relinquishing you. He used to boast about you to the boys at the station.'

I wasn't sure how to take his comments. I assumed he meant them as a compliment or an icebreaker. I changed the subject.

'What do you want to know?'

'How are you getting on? With the case, I mean. Have you got any leads yet?'

'I can't tell you much about it. George would have a fit. I have some good news, though. I talked to Noreen Ashcroft about the night of the murder.'

'Noreen?'

The pencil spinning increased in velocity.

'She told me she saw you there. How do you know her?'

'Um, I met her at Bertie Ashcroft's funeral. He was a large donor to police benevolent funds while he lived. We showed up in force to see him off. I saw her standing alone, weeping, and I went over to offer her my condolences. I ended up taking her back to her flat and having a cup of tea. She's a formidable woman, wasted on an old curmudgeon like Bertie. I'm glad she's enjoying his money now. He never let her buy anything while he was alive, you know.'

'So, you're friends.'

'I suppose you could say that. I visit her now and then and take her some fresh flowers or a bottle of Cava.'

'She claims to have seen somebody leave Blackwood's flat after you on the night of the murder.'

'Who?'

'Oh, we don't know yet. They were disguised in a mac and fedora.'

He laughed.

'How very Third Man that sounds.'

'If they find that person, you may be off the hook.'

'Yes, I would be, if they do.'

He seemed strangely unexcited about this revelation. I assumed the lack of sleep had dulled his brain.

'If you like I can tell you how Blackwood extracted confidential information from his victims to use for blackmail.'

'Really, it had me flummoxed. I had presumed he used hypnosis or something.'

'CCTV actually. The whole flat was rigged with cameras. Titania reviewed the footage to find people putting their passwords into their phones and wrote them down. Then, when people left their phones outside to meet with Blackwood in the inner sanctum, Titania raided their phones for information. You'd be amazed at what she came up with. Blackwood was blackmailing her too. Everyone was fair game to him.'

Terry scratched his head.

'No wonder,' he said. 'I couldn't imagine how he knew. Nobody on the force ever guessed what I was doing.'

He stared into my eyes, and I felt as if he was gauging my reaction to what he would say next.

'Ever guessed what?' I said, feeling prompted.

'My son became a thief to pay for his habit. At first we didn't notice, but it quickly became apparent that money would disappear from our wallets and knick-knacks from Belinda's cabinets. When questioned, he would fly into a rage and say we didn't love him, but, of course, we loved him too much. Soon, he started stealing from shops and eventually, when they blocked him from entering, he started selling his body. When I found out, I...'

He stared out at the waves and took several deep breaths before continuing.

'You've got to believe me. I was desperate. I thought he might be murdered by one of those men. I couldn't let that happen.'

'What did you do?' I asked, my heart in my mouth.

'I made him promise not to go out at night if I supplied him with drugs. I became his pusher. First, I tried to buy them on the street, but everyone in Sussex knows I'm a copper. Nobody would take my money. And then I remembered the evidence locker.'

I closed my eyes to shut out what he said next.

'I stole drugs from the dozens of bags taken on the street during stop and search, and raids on houses. There were so many of them. It was easy to take some from the larger bags and reseal them. Nobody noticed anything. I felt terrible, but I was keeping my son alive. More fool me. He left our house one night and never came back. I think he did it out of love. He didn't want me to risk my career for his addiction. He died of an overdose shortly after leaving home for good.'

'I'm so sorry. I don't know what to say.'

'Oh, it's not your fault. It's not anyone's fault. It just is. I had notes on my phone reminding me from which case's evidence bags I had taken drug samples, so I didn't take too much from any one raid or arrest. Blackwood must have got his hands on those notes using my password. I thought it was alchemy, but it was avarice.'

The knowledge seemed to calm him. He stopped twirling his pen and looked down at it as if surprised to find it in his hand.

'Where are you staying?' I said. 'Has your wife thrown you out?'

He shrugged.

'Is it so obvious? She resents my going to see Blackwood and trying to communicate with our son. She says I'm ruining her life. I've moved into the Travelodge for the time being. She may take me back if you prove me innocent, or she may not. I don't know.'

He rubbed his face with both hands and sighed.

'I shouldn't have asked you to help me. I've put you in an impossible position. George told me about your notebook. Can I help in any way?'

'Trust me and stay out of trouble. This case gets more complex by the minute.'

'Let's order something. I'm famished.'

Chapter 26

After DI Antrim had left the café, I wrote everything I could remember from my conversations with both him and Marge Dawson into my new A5 notebook. Marge's revelation that Titania and Raven were close friends added another tantalising clue to the mix. What could Raven be planning to reveal about Craig Latchford's relationship with Vivian Blackwood? I couldn't remember any signs of friendship between the two men. Admittedly, I never saw them together. Titania had been adamant about asking Latchford to leave when he turned up unexpectedly at the seance. And yet, Latchford had been hanging around smoking in the carpark beside Blackwood's building when I left the seance early. Smoking! The cigarette butt I had collected to throw out later was still in my handbag.

I tipped the contents out onto the table and sure enough the folded-up tissue had been lurking at the bottom, along with a couple of sweet wrappers and an old sticking plaster. I picked up the tissue with a clean napkin and wrapped it firmly in place, placing it in the inside zip pocket of my handbag. I patted my handbag to assure myself it was safely stored. I would give it to George as soon as possible. I had a feeling we had missed something important. I needed my notebook. Why had

Latchford changed his tune when I mentioned Ghita working in the planning department? Did he seriously think he could get planning permission past the council when they made him resign after the last debacle? Perhaps Raven had more information about his plans. I really needed to find her as soon as possible.

A young waiter stopped at my table.

'He already paid, you know. You don't have to search for your money.'

I thanked him and headed for the exit. I couldn't remember a case where I had been so confused. So many people had motives. But who snuck in later, using the service lift? I would ask George about people's alibis for that evening. If the murder had not been premeditated, sneaking into the flat after business hours in a mac and fedora seemed contradictory. And yet Flo had said it was a spur-of-the-moment crime. The murderer had not brought a weapon with them. They had used the first thing that came to hand. Or was it? Perhaps using a bust of the famous medium, Doris Stokes, had been deliberate and meant to send a message of some sort. Could another medium, resentful of Blackwood's success, have murdered him in a symbolic fashion?

I looked up and found myself at the door of Second Home. I had navigated there with remote sensing while my conscious mind worked on the murder. Mouse opened the door.

'Earth to Mum,' he said. 'Come in Tanya Bowe.'

I smiled at him.

'Sorry. I was on another planet.'

'Your hair looks dreamy. Marge is a magician.'

'And she rivals Roz for useful gossip. You'll never guess what she told me.'

'Oi,' said Roz. 'No one rivals me.'

'I meant today. She told me Titania is in contact with Raven, and Raven is planning to release a blog about Craig Latchford's relationship with Blackwood.'

'They were lovers?' said Ghita.

'No, their business relationship.'

'You've got to stop her,' said Roz. 'That girl has no concept of the havoc she will cause.'

'I could ring Titania now,' said Mouse. 'She'll talk to me. Anyway, I need to call her about passwords for Blackwood's computers. George wants me to help the police hack into Blackwood's files.'

'Is he going to pay you?'

'Yes, Mum. It's official police work.'

'Put the call on speakerphone,' said Ghita.

'Only if you swear not to speak. If she thinks anyone is listening, she won't talk. Oh, and, um, I might need to flirt a little, so don't laugh either.'

'Scout's honour,' I said.

'You were a girl guide,' said Roz. 'She only received one badge, for cooking sausages on an open fire.'

'That badge was for lighting the fire in the wilderness, not for cooking the sausages.'

'Whatever. I promise too.'

'And me,' said Ghita. 'Call her.'

We crowded around the counter. Mouse dialled Titania and propped the phone against the cash register. The ringtone echoed through the shop.

'Hello?'

Titania's voice sounded uncertain.

'T? It's me – Mouse.'

'Mouse? Oh… um, hi.'

She emitted a high-pitched laugh.

'You alright? You've gone quiet on the Minions group, so I thought I'd check in.'

'Seriously? Oh, that's… nice of you. I've been super stressed, honestly. Viv left me holding the bag when he got murdered, and now the fuzz reckon I helped him with the blackmail. It's peak,' said Titania.

'That's rough. I reckon I can help if you're up for it.'

'Course I am! I've no clue what I'm supposed to do.'

'I need the passwords to Blackwood's computer. From the office,' said Mouse.

'What? As if. No way… I'll get stitched up.'

'T, you've got to. This isn't a game. Someone Viv blackmailed probably killed him and then targeted Natalee Hedges. If they think you're sitting on his stuff, you could be next.'

'Me? Nah, I didn't even do anything. He sorted all that,' said Titania.

'Exactly. But if you show the fuzz you're helping, they'll go easier on you. It'd be even better if you came to the station with me. They need to hear your side of the story.'

A pause followed by a sigh.

'Would… would you, like, stay with me? Like, the whole time?'

'Yeah. I'll be there.'

A sharp voice cut in.

'Don't listen to him,' said Raven. 'His father's the DI.'

I scribbled 'Raven' on a receipt and held it up for Roz and Ghita to see, as well as Mouse. He nodded.

'Who's that?'

Silence. The sound of a muffled argument filtered through to the call. Finally, the other voice came on the line again.

'It's Raven, Titania's friend.'

'Raven? What are you even doing there? Didn't you nick my mum's notebook? We need that back. It's not safe. You're holding onto something someone might kill for,' said Mouse.

'I'm not going to the station with it,' said Raven. 'Your father would nick me.'

Mouse leant closer to the phone.

'Fine, but at least drop it at the shop. Mum's there. She won't kick off. She just needs her notebook back. Please, Raven. You're both in danger if you keep messing about. Look what happened to Natalee,' said Mouse.

'Is she over me borrowing it?' said Raven.

'Yeah,' said Mouse.

A long sigh came down the line.

'Okay. I'll bring the notebook,' said Raven.

'Good. I'll tell her you're coming,' said Mouse.

'I'll come to the station right now. Will you meet me outside?' said Titania.

'I'll be there in ten minutes,' said Mouse.

He rang off and pumped his fist at me.

'Well done, sweetheart. George will be so proud of you. Let's hope the files will tell us who murdered Blackwood and why.'

'Are you okay with Raven coming over? She was super rude to you last time.'

'If I get my notebook back, I might even make her a coffee.'

Chapter 27

After Mouse had left for the police station, Roz and Ghita bombarded me with questions. I told them about my visit to the hairdresser and feisty Marge Dawson, but I didn't tell them about DI Antrim's confession. I felt as if he had confided something sacred to me. They didn't need to know about his misdemeanours to understand the case. They both admired my hair and built up my ego first, and then they attacked me for being a rubbish friend. I took it gracefully, as I deserved all of it. Sometimes I get so wrapped up in cases, I forget what's important.

'I told you Craig Latchford was a prime suspect,' said Ghita. 'No one ever listens to me.'

'I'm sorry. I listened, but I got distracted by the flood of other possibilities,' I said.

'You hurt my feelings,' said Roz.

I rolled my eyes at her.

'You are the absolute top gossip in Seacastle no holds barred. Does that help?'

'For now. But one of these days I'm going to pit myself against Marge Dawson in a gossip-off. Only one of us can be the victor.'

'Do you think DI Antrim is guilty?' asked Ghita.

'The evidence seems to point to Craig Latchford.'

'She didn't ask you about the evidence,' said Roz. 'You sound like George.'

'He had a powerful motive. And people can do dreadful things in a fit of fury. I can't discount him yet. I think there's something about what happened that night he hasn't told the police yet.'

We didn't have to wait long for Raven Huxley to turn up. She sidled into the shop dressed in a long black cloak. She had coloured beads braided into her waist-length black hair. If her face hadn't been so pinched with hate, she would have been an attractive young woman. As it was, I had to swallow my fury at her stealing my beloved notebook as I knew it was the only way of getting it back.

'I'm here,' she said, gesticulating at Roz and Ghita who were gobsmacked by this apparition. 'But you'll have to get rid of the other two if you want me to talk to you.'

I nodded my assent. Roz sighed and dragged Ghita upstairs with her. I could hear them moving chairs next to the banisters so they could hear better. Raven pulled a stool up to the counter.

'I'm returning the notebook you lent me.'

Lent her? What a massive cheek that girl had! She took it out of her miniature rucksack and dropped it on the counter. I picked the notebook up and restrained myself from kissing it. Instead, I put it in the back pocket of my jeans.

'Thanks,' I said. 'I didn't know you were friends with Titania.'

'We're cousins. We've known each other since we were babies.'

'Seriously? You must be so worried about her. I don't know how you deal with it.'

She tilted her head to one side and drew her eyebrows together.

'What do you mean?'

'Oh, I thought you knew. The police think Titania's next on the murderer's list. They're working on the premise that he's killing for revenge. Blackwood couldn't have blackmailed anyone without Titania's help.'

'Who told you that?'

'She did. We know all about her stealing the passwords and information from people's phones. Did you help her? It must have been so fascinating to find out people's secrets and watch them suffer.'

'I don't know what you mean. I'm a victim too. Or at least I nearly was. They wanted our land for their dodgy project.'

A chill ran down my back, and the hairs on my arms stood on end.

'What sort of project?'

'Blackwood and his business partner wanted to build a housing estate outside Lancing.'

'Do you know the name of his partner?'

'Are you, like, literally stupid or something? Craig Latchford. I thought you'd met him the day—'

'Oh yes, I forgot about that. Please go on.'

'Yeah. My sister and I literally own the land where they were planning on constructing the buildings. She couldn't sign the land away without me. So Latchford tried to put pressure on us. As if.'

She shook her head.

'What's this got to do with the investigation into Blackwood's death?'

'After we wouldn't give him the land, he literally left Latchford holding the baby. The investors dropped out when they discovered the company didn't own the land. Latchford's political comeback will be in tatters, like, when they discover he owes money to half of West Sussex. Blackwood literally bankrupted him.'

'So you think Latchford murdered Blackwood?'

She rolled her eyes at me.

'I know he did.'

'Do you have proof?'

'I literally just gave you the proof.'

'That's the motive. I meant evidence, forensics, that sort of thing.'

'I thought you were, like, investigating the case. Aren't you supposed to do the proving?'

I had to admit she had a point.

'Do you have any documents backing up your story?'

'No, but my sister does.'

'What's your sister's name?'

'Robin Dixon.'

I laughed. The memory of the stroppy woman at Ghita's step class was still fresh.

'What's so funny?'

'Nothing. Do you think I could speak to her?'

'As if. She's in hiding.'

'From whom?'

'Craig Latchford, of course. You're not much of a detective, are you? The ones on the telly get it right in an hour.'

'I do my best. Tell your sister she should go to the police if she knows what's good for her.'

'We don't like coppers,' she said.

'They might be about to save your lives. Can I have your number?' I said.

'Give me your phone and I'll key it in. I don't have all day, like you do.'

I handed her my phone, standing in front of the door to prevent her from taking that too. She smirked at me when she saw what I had done. She tapped in her number and handed me the phone. I pressed dial as a precaution, and the phone rang in her handbag.

'You're not as dumb as you look,' she said. 'I'm going now. Don't try to stop me.'

She scampered around me and out of the door before I could ask her any more questions. I sat behind the counter musing on the new information. Roz and Ghita thundered down the stairs.

'I told you,' said Ghita. 'It's Latchford. He's the murderer. You should have listened to me in the first place.'

'He's certainly got a motive,' I said.

'And opportunity,' said Roz. 'You saw him there yourself.'

'And he didn't need the means. He just picked up the bust in Blackwood's office and dented his head with it,' said Ghita.

It all seemed to fit. If what Raven had told me turned out to be correct, we had a new and totally credible motive for Blackwood's murder. Latchford certainly had the physique for bludgeoning people with blunt objects. And the temper. But did he have the opportunity? How did he get into Blackwood's flat after everyone had gone? Was he the person Noreen Ashcraft spotted using the service lift?

Of course, these suppositions depended on Raven Huxley's story being true. She struck me as shallow and vindictive. Was she just looking for a good story for her blog? I needed Mouse to research her and find out if she and her sister really owned that land. Most of all, I needed to talk to Latchford without him suspecting my motive. I remembered our first conversation and smiled to myself. If you want to catch a big fish, you need the correct bait, and I had just the thing. As long as she didn't get all huffy and refuse; Ghita Chowdhury, the key to the planning office of Seacastle Council.

Chapter 28

Raven Huxley was right about my being stupid. About half an hour after she left Second Home, and while we were still discussing the implications of Latchford's involvement in Blackwood's murder, she published an article about Ocean Drive, the project planned by Latchford and Blackwood. She detailed how they tried to swindle her and her sister and insinuated nefarious goings on at the council and in Blackwood's office. She linked the project's failure to Blackwood's murder. I had completely forgotten to forbid her from publishing anything about the case. I could almost hear her cackling somewhere in a corner. As usual, I was the last to know about Raven's blog, until my phone rang. It was George apoplectic with rage.

'What the bloody hell is going on, Tan? Mouse told me you were dealing with the blogger person, but she has just published an article about Blackwood and Latchford online. Tell her to take it down right now. I want you down at the station right now before the case is destroyed by prejudicial information being available to the public. Can you bring her with you?'

'She left about half an hour ago. I have her phone number, but I don't think she's likely to answer.'

'What a train wreck! Come now. Flo has received some more results from the forensics, and as much as I'd like her to be wrong, it looks as if the blogger may have a point.'

'I'll be there shortly.'

I hung up to find Ghita and Roz staring at me.

'She's published the article. I forgot to tell her not to.'

'If she had an ounce of sense, that would have been obvious,' said Roz.

'George sounded cross. You'd better go straight there. We'll shut the shop,' said Ghita. 'Bring a cake with you. That might take the edge off his anger.'

'Good idea.'

I put a chocolate cake into a cake tin and hurried to the station with my heart in my mouth. Honestly, call yourself a sleuth, Tanya Bowe? Sally Wright at the reception desk gave me a sympathetic smile when I burst through the station doors, panting from my accelerated stride. I held on to my side, wincing as I waited for the stitch to dissipate.

'He's in the meeting room with DS Brennan and Flo,' she said.

'Is steam coming out of his ears?'

'Every orifice,' she said, buzzing me through.

I tried to slow my heart rate as I walked down the corridor to the meeting room. I had no control over what Raven Huxley did. She was an adult.

George looked up at me from his habitual pile of paper. He didn't do tablets. A long silence ensued. I gave Flo a pleading glance.

'Shall I talk about forensics?' she said.

George growled something at her.

'I'll take that as a yes,' she said. 'Well, we have received results from the fingerprints taken at the scene of the murder. Of particular interest were the fingerprints on a glass we found under Blackwood's body. To be honest, an assumption was made that it was his glass, and we didn't put a rush on the results because of budget constraints.'

George tapped his fingers on the table.

'Anyway, to cut a long story short, we found Blackwood's prints on the glass, and we also found two other sets of prints, one of which was Titania Grafton's.'

'She probably poured him a glass of water,' said Joe Brennan. 'The fridge was beside her desk.'

'And to whom did the other prints belong?' I asked.

'We're not sure. There's another DNA on the glass too, but neither is in the police database,' said Flo.

'Did you take Latchford's prints to use for elimination?' I said.

'No, only the people who attended the seance that afternoon and had paid sums of money into Blackwood's account.'

'Ah, well, I'm not sure if anyone mentioned this, but Latchford came in just before the seance began and demanded to see Blackwood. Titania sent him away with a flea in his ear. When I left the seance early, I found Latchford having a cigarette in the car park. He did not engage with me until I told him Ghita was a friend of mine. He became quite chummy when he heard she had transferred to the council planning office.'

'Why didn't you tell us about this?'

'Because nobody mentioned him in the context of Blackwood's murder. I had totally forgotten until Raven mentioned him. And, oh, wait.'

I rummaged through my handbag and found the folded-up tissue, which I handed to Flo.

'I picked up this cigarette butt after Latchford threw it on the floor. I had intended to put it in a bin, but I found it still in my bag today. I think it's uncontaminated except for clean tissue.'

I pushed it across the table to Flo. She did not pick it up immediately.

'We can check it against the unknown DNA,' she said. 'I'd like to bet it belongs to Latchford.'

'There's something else,' said Joe. 'Blackwood's watch had fallen off in the ambulance and was only spotted yesterday. It stopped at a quarter past seven, so we can now create a detailed timeline for the murder.'

'It's a massive advance in the case. Blackwood had the air conditioning up high to make the atmosphere in the consulting room feel chilly and spooky. It cooled his body quicker than usual, so I found it hard to pin down the time of death at the scene,' said Flo.

'It should also enable us to check alibis and eliminate suspects from our inquiries,' said George.

'Fantastic. Let me know if I can help.'

'You've already helped enough with my case. What's in the tin?'

'Chocolate cake,' I said. 'Ghita sent you emergency rations.'

He beamed.

'Some good news at last.'

He pressed the button on the intercom.

'Any chance of a pot of tea in here? We're gasping. Oh and bring small plates and a knife.'

'How well does Ghita know Craig Latchford?' asked Joe.

'He used to ignore her when she worked in logistics, but he knows who she is,' I said.

'I've got a cunning plan.'

George raised an eyebrow.

'Seriously?'

'It's not as cunning as—'

'No Blackadder in here. Only Blackwood.'

Joe pouted.

'Anyway,' he said. 'What if Ghita asks Latchford to meet her to talk about planning permission for Ocean Drive? She could use a wire.'

I feigned horror, although I knew Ghita would be ecstatic to carry out a mission like that. The best way to persuade George was to oppose it. I know him well.

'Bait? You want to use Ghita as bait? You must be off your rocker. How can you even consider that?' I said, feeling myself redden with fake indignation.

'She'd be perfectly safe,' said George. 'We'd be close by.'

'You think this is a good plan too?'

'I do. You can't take it personally. Ghita is the one who must decide if she will step into the lion's den.'

Personally, I could see her accepting without a qualm.

'But that man may have murdered two people,' I said.

'One,' said Joe. 'So far.'

'What about Natalee Hedges?'

'Her husband has been arrested,' said George. 'He hit her with a hammer. The forensics boys found brain matter on one in the tool shed. He didn't bother to clean it properly. His fingerprints are all over it.'

I felt sick.

'Her husband? We did this. We should have taken her away from there immediately.'

George shook his head.

'Natalee Hedges and her husband were well known to the police. She had been offered help many times, but she refused it. She believed she could get away by herself at a time of her choosing.'

'He's being held at Brighton Police Station,' said Joe. 'He'll stand trial for murder. They have damning forensics and circumstantial to back it up.'

'Where does DI Antrim stand in all this?' I asked.

'We can't rule him out, but if I were a betting man, I'd be putting the house on Craig Latchford for the murder of Blackwood.'

'And you want to dangle Ghita in front of him like a juicy worm in front of a voracious salmon?'

'Yup,' said Joe. 'Ghita will love it. She's smart and feisty. He won't get the better of her.'

Something in his tone made me look up. The tips of his ears had turned pink. Had our junior DI developed a crush? I racked my brain. Didn't he have a girlfriend? Policemen didn't travel the easiest road with their relationships. I should know. All those late nights and missed events make for common breakups between partners. Sally Wright would tell me if I asked her. I scribbled in my notebook.

'At least you got that back,' said Flo. 'You must have felt as if you were missing an arm.'

'Are you insinuating I have serious notebook attachment issues?'

'I'm not insinuating anything. I'm stating a fact.'

The door opened, and Sally Wright came in with a tray of mugs and side plates.

'Time to get down to business,' said George. 'Release the cake.'

Chapter 29

Rumours about the availability of one of Ghita's famous cakes spread through the station like wildfire. Luckily, I had anticipated the demand and cut small slices to give everyone a chance. This caused grumbling among certain staffers who thought their seniority entitled them to larger slices. Mouse turned up just in time to nab the last slice. He cleaned the bottom of the tin of stray blobs of icing with his finger.

'Yum. Ghita's cakes make life so much sweeter,' he said.

I caught Joe smirking. He pretended to have something fascinating on the screen of his tablet.

'Have you found anything interesting?' asked George. 'Aside from the cake.'

'Blackwood's computer is a goldmine of information. He saved every payment, every secret, every email in beautifully labelled files. There's no doubt Blackwood ran a one-man crime syndicate. The question is – did it kill him?'

'Have you looked at your phone recently?' I said.

'No, I've had my nose glued to the screen for hours. Why?'

'Raven Huxley has published another blog. This time about Craig Latchford.'

'Let me read it.'

Mouse sank into a plastic chair and took out his phone, scrolling at warp speed. Then he stopped. His eyes opened wide, and he swore under his breath. After a couple of minutes, he looked up to find everyone waiting for his reaction.

'Wow, that's brutal,' he said. 'It looks as if we have a new prime suspect.'

'What do the files say?' said Joe.

'Blackwood was a wealthy man. He blackmailed many of his clients for small or large sums, depending on what they could afford. He could have bought a villa in Spain and retired without ever working again. I guess he got greedy.'

'Does it contain details of his relationship with Craig Latchford?' asked George.

'I've just read most of that file. Latchford sent him menacing letters. Mind you, Emily Carradine did too.'

'The teacher?' said Joe.

'Yes. She sent a letter threatening to expose him as a fraud if he didn't stop blackmailing his clients, including her.'

'Did it have any effect?'

'Her payments stopped after the letter, so maybe they spoke and he agreed to leave her alone.'

'She told me she went to talk to Natalee Hedges to ask her to stop working with Blackwood,' I said. 'But that doesn't seem so important now Natalee's husband has been charged with murdering her.'

'I can't see her as a murderer,' said Mouse. 'She's living in fear of being arrested because of the letter she sent. We could pull her in for a chat, I suppose.'

'And who asked you?' said George. 'I decide who we interview and who we don't.'

Mouse gave a sheepish grin.

'Sorry, Dad. I forgot. Blame Tanya.'

'He already does,' I said.

'Let's go back to Latchford,' said Joe. 'Can you find any evidence of the deal to which Raven Huxley was referring?'

'There's no shortage of paperwork about it,' said Mouse. 'In their email correspondence, Blackwood complains to Latchford that Robin Huxley has refused to hand over their land. Latchford is blaming Blackwood and saying he will be bankrupted if Blackwood doesn't keep up his end of the deal.'

'No wonder Latchford was in a temper when he came to see Blackwood at his office,' I said.

'Did he tell you anything about the deal when you spoke to him in the car park?' asked Joe.

'No, he didn't mention it. He engaged only when I mentioned Ghita worked in the planning department.'

'We have the cigarette butt now to test for his DNA, but I would like to place him in Blackwood's office. We need his fingerprints too,' said George.

'If Tanya didn't touch the butt with her fingers, I'm likely to find those on the same cigarette end,' said Flo.

'Can you expedite that work?'

'I can start now if you like.'

'Great,' said George. 'If we can place Latchford in Blackwood's office that night, we may have our murderer.'

'What about DI Antrim?' said Joe.

'He doesn't deny having been there on the night Blackwood was murdered. But Noreen Ashcroft told Tanya somebody left after him, wearing a mac and a fedora,' said George.

'We need to concentrate on that suspect,' said Joe. 'I'll get uniform to go house to house and rustle up a sighting.'

Mouse scratched his head.

'What if that was Titania herself? We have only her word about DI Antrim being the last one in the office. What if it were her? She could easily have kept the glass from a meeting or seance and planted it under Blackwood's body to sow confusion.'

Someone knocked on the door of the meeting room and handed George a printout.

'It's Blackwood's up-to-date bank statement,' he said. 'The one we had was missing the last transactions as they were made on the weekend.'

He placed the papers on his desk and ran his finger down the columns while we all waited on tenterhooks. George's eyes widened, and then almost stood out on stalks.

'Any revelations, guv?' said Joe.

'He emptied his account. Two million pounds. Just like that.'

'Where did he send it?' asked Mouse. 'Do you want me to trace it?'

'It's a Swiss bank account, I think.'

I slapped my forehead.

'Oh, it all makes sense now.'

'What does?' said Joe.

'When I attended the seance with Roz, Blackwood said he would soon leave for the next world. Everyone assumed he was predicting his own death, and when he was murdered, that solidified his reputation as a medium.'

'How did he know though?' said Mouse.

George rolled his eyes.

'I'd say it was obvious. Joe, what does it tell you?'

'He planned to fake his own death and do a runner with all his cash. Maybe someone found out?'

'Latchford?' I asked.

'Possibly. But the last payment made from the account before he emptied it is a transfer of two hundred thousand pounds in the name of Craig Latchford,' said George.

'Why would Latchford have murdered him after being paid so much money?' asked Joe.

'But he wouldn't have known about the transfer until Monday,' I said. 'Maybe he killed him in a fit of anger before Blackwood could show him the proof that he had sent it?'

'We need to get Latchford in for questioning. I'll let you know what he says,' said George.

'Can't I be present?'

'No. Not this time. And we won't be needing Ghita either.'

I resisted the temptation to check Joe's facial expression.

'Good luck,' I said, as I left them puzzling over the accounts, but I don't think they heard me.

I met Flo on her way back from the AFIS (Automatic Fingerprint Identification System) room where the machine that checked the fingerprints was kept. She had a frown on her face.

'I'm not at all sure about the forensics right now. Everything is pointing to someone different.'

'At least you have a firm time for the murder. That should help, right?'

'Yeah. I guess so.'

'Have you heard anything from the Met about that job?'

'Not yet. I thought it was nailed on, but now they are coming up with excuses.'

'Maybe it's not meant to be. I'd hate to lose you. And you know what Mouse thinks.'

'I know. But Seacastle is such a backwater, and I'm ready to spread my wings. Working for the Met would be the pinnacle of my career.'

'I'll keep my fingers crossed for you.'

Once outside, I texted Mouse to ask if he was coming home too. He told me to wait and came out five minutes later.

'How did it go with Titania today?' I said.

'Pretty well, really. She stayed all day. I expected her to leave with me now, but she went back for her phone.'

'Honestly, you lot and your phones. Soon humans will be born with them attached.'

'At least we won't lose them then.'

Chapter 30

After all my work on the case, I felt disappointed not to watch George and Joe reel in Craig Latchford. He seemed to me to be a thoroughly objectionable man, a liar and a bully who didn't care who got in his way. I could easily imagine him losing his temper with Blackwood and bludgeoning him to death with the nearest blunt object. However, the large transfer made by Blackwood around the time of his murder put a spanner in the works.

Mouse and Harry had planned to go to the Shanty for lunch and to watch a football match, but I wasn't in the mood. I stayed home watching daytime TV and trying to persuade Hades to hang out with me on the sofa. My phone pinged at me, and I picked it up, wary of scam calls ruining my mood. A message from Helen, asking me to come to lunch and give her the lowdown on the Blackwood case. I winced as I remembered why I had been avoiding her. She couldn't have been impressed by my ratting her out about seeing Blackwood. She'd probably let me off if I gave her enough gory details about the case. Since it had basically been sewn up, I didn't feel bad about telling her most things. One fact I could be sure of was that Helen did not murder Blackwood. Her hero worship had been toned down by the discovery he had been blackmailing his clients, but not as much as I had expected.

'He must have been desperate for money,' she said, ushering me into the kitchen. 'Maybe his mother's in a care home. You know how expensive they can be.'

I raised an eyebrow at this convoluted effort to sanitise her former hero.

'He spied on people's private messages on their phones and asked them for money to keep quiet about them. He was hardly a paragon of virtue.'

'Well, I didn't know that when I went to see him. I thought I could contact Mummy one last time.'

'I don't know why you needed to,' I said. 'You are her reincarnation on Earth in almost every way. And I look identical to her. She hasn't gone away. She has just gifted her genetics to us in different ways. You remind me of her every time I see you.'

She stared at me.

'Really? Because I can see her sitting right opposite me. I was a little jealous, to tell you the truth, of how much you looked like her.'

'And me of you. You sound so like her, and you act as if her spirit has possession of you.'

'Then we haven't really lost her, have we?'

'We are her,' I said. 'She won't ever die. Especially when Olivia is another clone of her Granny.'

Helen's eyes were sparkling at this point.

'I don't know why I needed to see a clairvoyant when you live two streets away. Do you fancy pork pie and salad? I've got some new potatoes on the boil.'

It didn't take long to throw a salad together and to make a honey mustard dressing for it. Soon we were sitting at the table about to tuck in. Helen helped herself to salad. The front door opened and slammed at the same moment. Helen jumped up.

'George? We're in here, darling. Do you fancy some lunch?'

George blew in like a storm cloud over the Andes, extinguishing the cordial atmosphere and casting gloom over our sisterly meal. He plonked himself down into a seat at the table, while Helen bustled about getting him a place setting. He glared at me.

'What are you staring at?' he said.

'I thought you'd be in a good mood after the interview. Didn't Latchford turn up?'

'Oh, he turned up all right. He had all the right answers.'

'Why don't you tell us, dear?' said Helen. 'I'm sure Tanya wants to hear this.'

'I need food first.'

We served ourselves and ate in almost total silence. The food was delicious, but I could hardly swallow it. My throat had tightened with anticipation.

Finally, George had emptied his plate. He laid down his fork and cleared his throat.

'Latchford came in for an interview this morning, cocky as you like. I can't bear the man.'

'Join the crowd,' I said.

He scowled at me for interrupting him. I pretended to zip up my mouth. He nodded.

'Anyway, he didn't deny any of it. He told us he'd been pals with Blackwood since they were at junior school together. They've always backed each other up with their scams no matter what. He admitted to being furious with Blackwood after he failed to persuade the Huxley sisters to part with their land to build Ocean Drive. But Blackwood had promised to wire him the two hundred grand to make it right. He told us the money had arrived in his bank the Monday after the murder.'

'But that doesn't mean he's telling the truth,' I said. 'If the money didn't get to his account until Monday, maybe he murdered Blackwood in a fury before he realised he had been paid?'

'That's what we thought. But Mr Chen put paid to our theory. Craig Latchford bought himself a Chinese takeaway at seven o'clock on Saturday evening. Mr Chen checked the CCTV for us and sent us an image of Latchford ordering chow mein at seven-fifteen.'

'So he didn't kill Latchford? But who else could it have been?'

'We're right back at square one,' said George. 'I can't believe it.'

'Isn't Joe working on the timelines?'

'Yes, but we have to re-interview everyone and verify the alibis. It's an awful lot of work.'

'I'm sorry, darling,' said Helen. 'You must be disappointed. Would you like some pudding?'

George's face lit up.

'What is there?'

'Eton Mess.'

'Excellent. Yes, please.'

'Me too.'

I left soon after lunch and went straight to the shop. I needed to distract myself from my disappointment. Roz took one look at me and made me a sweet latte.

'What's up?' she said, passing me the steaming mug of coffee.

'This case is getting me down. There are too many suspects and not enough evidence. I promised DI Antrim I'd find out who murdered Vivian Blackwood, but I've failed miserably.'

She frowned at me.

'Honestly, I know you think you're Jessica Fletcher, but you need to be more realistic. You have provided George and his team with some valuable clues. They would be lost without you. But they are professionals. In the end, it doesn't matter whether you think Terry is guilty. George will decide if he has sufficient evidence to ask for a prosecution, not you.'

'But the prime suspect has an alibi. We're back to square one.'

'No, you're not. You're just feeling defeated right now. You've lost a battle, not the war.'

'But I don't know what to do next.'

'I'd go on a clearance if I were you. Harry popped in earlier looking for you. He had a call from an old woman in Lancing asking for him to clear out her house tomorrow.'

'Really? That would be wonderful. I'm so worn out with this case. But can you look after the shop for me?'

'I've already called Ghita. I can do the morning, and she'll do the afternoon when she's finished her lunchtime shift at Surfusion.'

'That woman is a dynamo. Where does she get all her energy?'

'I don't know, but we should bottle it and sell it to the jaded population of Seacastle.'

'Thanks Roz. I really appreciate it.'

'I'm the one who should thank you. I don't know who killed that horrible man, but I never would have been free of him if you hadn't warned me about him. Let's hope we've heard the last of it.'

Chapter 31

We set out later than usual the next morning. Having had a bottle of wine while watching a movie, neither of us felt like getting up earlier to make our usual bacon sandwiches.

'We can eat when we get to Lancing,' said Harry. 'Why don't we go to the West Beach deli and pick up some grub for brunch? I'll make us a flask of tea.'

'Perfect. We can walk around the lagoon and sit on the beach.'

I dragged on a pair of chinos and an old denim shirt and brushed my hair back into a bun. I put on a pair of what we used to call plimsolls, although Mouse referred to them as daps, and took a couple of deep breaths. I couldn't help feeling depressed about Latchford wriggling off the hook. He was almost as unpleasant as Blackwood and merited prison time too with his dodgy behaviour. Under election law, he couldn't even be deselected as a councillor until the next election when other people could contest his seat. It seemed ludicrous, but Ghita assured me it was correct. I looked at myself in the mirror and forced myself to smile and be positive about the clearance before going downstairs.

Soon we were motoring along the road on the quick trip to Lancing. Mrs Ruth Waters lived in a southwest facing house on a road near the railway station. I coveted one of these neat terraced houses, and I couldn't wait to go inside one and nose around. We were lucky to find a parking space almost directly in front of the house. Harry knocked on the door, and a tiny old lady, who reminded me of Gladys, Joy's mother, answered it. Her left leg had a plaster cast on it, and she had a pair of crutches to help her walk.

'You're the clearance people? Won't you come in? I'm afraid I've got bad news for you.'

Harry and I followed her precarious progress down the short hall into a picture-perfect sitting room, which looked as if we had stepped back into the nineteen forties. My heart skipped a beat as I noticed the treasures in full view. An old Bakelite radio set sat on a beautifully polished maple sideboard.

'Wow. Your sitting room is gorgeous,' I said. 'I'm speechless.'

She smiled.

'It took me twenty years to get it just so, you know. A work of art.'

Harry picked up a photograph of a handsome young man with a handlebar moustache, which took pride of place on the mantlepiece over the tiled fireplace.

'Your son?' he asked.

'My husband. It was taken in the Far East somewhere. He was drafted and sent to police the skies when we were first married. He's dead now, of course.'

'I'm sorry to hear that. He looks like just the sort of bloke I would have liked to meet.'

'You're ex-service too? You've got the swagger,' she said.

'There's nothing wrong with your eyesight, Mrs Waters,' I said.

'I've always liked a man in uniform.'

'Enough about me,' said Harry. 'What can we do for you?'

'That's the trouble. There's nothing you can do for me. My son wants to put me in a care home. I made it easy for him by breaking my ankle last month.'

She took a linen handkerchief from her sleeve and dabbed her eyes with it.

'But you want to stay here?' I asked.

'Of course. Who'd want to leave this comfortable home and live with a bunch of deaf, bickering old folk? I'm blissfully happy where I am now.'

'I would be too,' said Harry. 'Why does he want you to move?'

'I can't get to the shops or up stairs with this broken ankle. He says I'm too old to cope and have to move somewhere I'll be safe. But I'll die if they make me go there. This is my home.'

'He called us to come and clear the house while you're still here?' I said. 'That seems unusual.'

'He said I could choose the things I want for my room in the care home and I had to give you everything else. I don't know what to do.'

'Does he have a lasting power of attorney to act for you?' I asked. 'Because otherwise he can't tell you what to do. He's trying to bully you into leaving.'

'Well, I know he doesn't mean to, but that's what it feels like. He keeps telling me I'll be all alone in this house and no one will help me.'

'Are you a veteran too?' asked Harry.

'Actually, I am. I used to be a nurse in the RAF.'

'You need to join the Veterans Club in Seacastle. They have legal advisors and can arrange home help for you. You don't need to leave your home if you don't want to.'

'But will they talk to him about it? I find him intimidating, and I can't say no to him. He always was a spoilt child, and I'm afraid he has improved little as an adult. I—'

A loud knock on the door interrupted our chat. Harry held up his hand and smiled.

'I'll get it,' he said.

He walked to the front door and opened it.

'Are you the clearance person?' said a young man's voice. 'Why haven't you got started yet?'

His belligerent tone of voice made Ruth cringe, and I saw fear in her eyes. I guessed the voice belonged to her son, and I wondered how she had hurt her ankle.

'We're talking,' said Harry. I could almost see his chest puffing out as he measured the physical threat. If the son had any sense, he would lose the attitude.

'Talking?' said the voice. 'I pay you to act.'

'As far as I'm aware, you haven't offered to pay us anything.'

'But you get all this free furniture. What more do you expect?'

'I expect a little respect.'

'You need to earn it first.'

I bit my lip to stifle a guffaw. This guy had to be blind if he hadn't noticed Harry's quiet threat. I heard a muffled squeak and a thud. I guessed Harry had shoved him against the wall.

'If I were you, sonny, I'd pick my battles. Your mother is not moving. She's happy here, and you should do everything in your power to let her stay. Perhaps you could put in a stairlift? You look as if you can afford it.'

'And what are you going to do about it?'

'I'm going to give her my phone number, and next time you try to force her to move, I'm going to introduce you to some friends of mine from the SAS. They're bored as hell being back home in Blighty. They'd like some practice in hand to hand, if you know what I mean.'

'There's no need to threaten me. My mother is a stubborn old bat. She'd be much happier in a home.'

'Why don't you let her decide that?'

'I don't like being threatened.'

'Neither do I. I suggest you take my advice and let her live here in peace. She's earned it.'

'And what do you get out of it?'

'Peace of mind.'

'Peace of mind? Are you some sort of nutter?'

'Possibly. But if I'm unstable, you need to avoid overexciting me, don't you?'

A silence, during which I imagined them having a staring match.

'It's a bloody liberty,' said the voice, and footsteps echoed down the pavement.

The front door closed, and Harry came back into the sitting room.

'Well, that's all sorted then. We'll leave you to it,' he said.

'I don't know how to thank you,' said Ruth.

'Put my number into your address book,' said Harry, 'And use it if you need to.'

Ruth tried to persuade us to stay for a cup of tea, but I had already decided to take a break on the beach of the Lancing Lagoon. We left her beaming in her armchair, watching Countdown and knitting a beanie for her granddaughter.

The West Beach deli was on the corner only a hop, skip and jump from where we were parked, but Harry drove us there anyway.

'You never know if Junior might decide to let down our tyres,' he said.

We parked on a side road and entered the deli through the front door. A gleaming glass cabinet stuffed full of delicious sandwiches and smoothies sat beside the wooden counter, behind which was a blackboard covered in tempting suggestions. I chose a large ham and cheese croissant and a fresh orange juice. Harry went for the bacon and brie baguette. He also bought a couple of chocolate brownies for dessert. We walked across the road and crossed the new bridge over the lagoon towards the beach. The flask bumped against my leg as I crossed the dunes onto the pebbled beach. Coloured beach huts lined the shore, giving it a picture postcard look.

'What about just here?' said Harry, gesticulating at a slight bowl in the sand surrounded by sea grasses.

'Perfect. It should be sheltered from the breeze too.'

We sat on the sand and divided the spoils. I poured us cups of tea from the flask, and we sipped them with sighs of appreciation. I tried to eat slowly, but my croissant was so delicious I couldn't help scoffing it. Harry's baguette disappeared in quick order too. He rolled up his jacket and lay back against it on the sand.

'I'm hungover. I think I'll take a nap. Don't let me sleep too long.'

'Okay, sweetheart. I'm going to sit here and think.'

'About the case? You need to forget it for a couple of days. Your unconscious brain will work on it and come up with a solution.'

'Did I tell you how proud I was of you standing up to that horrible man?'

'Don't change the subject.'

Within seconds, the gentle sound of snoring rose from his body. As soon as he was asleep, I took out my notebook. I knew Harry was right about leaving the case to marinate, but something was nagging at me and I had to check. I flipped back through the pages to my first talk with DI Antrim. He had been speaking rapidly, and I had made some almost incomprehensible notes about it. I struggled to make out some sentences, frowning at the scrawl as if it would clarify through narrowed eyes. I read the part about him meeting Blackwood and then about his shock at the murder. I had to read it twice before the penny dropped. My chest tightened, and I felt sick. I shook Harry awake.

'I'm really sorry, sweetheart, but we've got to go back to Blackwood's building. I need to check something with Noreen Ashcroft.'

He rolled his eyes at me.

'Seriously?'

'I'm afraid I may have cracked the case.'

'That was quick.'

'I didn't do it on purpose. I think Noreen told me porkies about the night of the murder.'

'Let's go.'

Chapter 32

As we headed back to the van, my brain was doing cartwheels in my skull. DI Antrim had expressed horror that someone had bludgeoned Blackwood to death. But how did he know what the killer had done? The information had not been released so early in the case, and George would never make a suspect privy to such information, even if he was a police officer. I had a dreadful sinking feeling in my stomach that made my croissant as heavy as a cannonball. I tried to stay calm, but it seemed the truth had been staring me in the face. Why on earth did Terry beg me to exonerate him when he knew I would not? I had to speak to Noreen. Without her alibi, DI Antrim would be nailed on for the murder. She had claimed to have seen someone else taking the service lift from her floor after Terry Antrim had left Blackwood's flat. What if she had been mistaken?

The forensic team had found no evidence of an unidentified person at the scene. Nor had they matched the owners of any fingerprints on the outside of the lift to any of the suspects. Either Noreen had got it wrong, or the murder squad was back to square one with their investigation. I couldn't help feeling like I had missed something. After our prime suspect had produced an unbreakable alibi for the time of the murder, the leads had all gone cold. And yet, Antrim himself had described the murder scene to me without an attempt at hiding the truth, but maybe a chat with Noreen would clarify the situation.

Harry and I drove parallel to the promenade with the windows down. The sea breeze, heavy with the smell of rotting seaweed, blew through the interior of the car and whipped up the papers lying on the dashboard. Harry slowed down to stop them from flying out of the window. Little white horses rushed onto the shore, leaving small ripples in the sand and wetting the legs of the children paddling there. I tried to slow my heart rate, which had been sky high with the stress of the case, mostly caused by ignoring the truth, which now threatened to drown out all the theories. I just didn't want to believe it.

Harry did not want to come with me to see Noreen, in case she felt intimidated. He stayed in the van, looking at the sea, with Led Zeppelin playing on the cassette machine. I entered the building and walked to the lift, pressing the button and waiting as it descended with majestic slowness from the top floor. The doors opened in front of me, but instead of entering the lift, I changed my mind and headed for the back of the building down a narrow corridor. The service lift sat at the end with its doors shut and an *Out of Service* notice stuck on with masking tape. I pressed the call button in the vain hope the doors would open, but the lift sat solid and silent in front of me, giving no secrets away. I tried to slip my fingers between the doors, but they were sealed shut. I heard a cough behind me. A squat woman, who looked as if she should have a cigarette dangling from her lip, gave me a once over.

'What are you doing?' she asked.

'Oh, I was wondering when the service lift will be working. A friend of mine is thinking of moving out.'

'That lift hasn't worked for months, ducks. I don't think it's been running all year, now that I remember.'

I frowned.

'Are you sure? My friend said she used it last month.'

'Your friend is hallucinating. I'm sure it has been broken down since Christmas. Who do you know that lives in this building?'

'Noreen Ashcroft. She lives on the fifth floor. I was hoping to visit her today.'

'You're not much of a friend, are you?' she said, drawing her eyebrows together.

'What do you mean?'

'Well, she's been taken ill with a stroke last week. She's in the hospice now. They don't think she'll survive. How come you don't know that?'

'Um, I've had a bereavement in the family, and I've been distracted trying to organise the funeral. I'm quite upset by the whole thing to tell you the truth.'

A real tear ran down my cheek as I struggled to control myself.

'I'm sorry. I didn't mean to be harsh. That's just my way. But if I were you, I'd toddle along to the hospice as fast as you can. She'll be coming out of there feet first, if you ask me.'

'What about her dog?' I asked. 'Priscilla? What's happening to her?'

'They took her into the kennels for now. I expect they'll re-home her.'

Even though Priscilla the Poo-covered Pomeranian was the last dog on earth that I would allow in my house, I felt desperately sad for Noreen, stuck in the hospice without her.

'What's the name of the hospice?' I asked.

'I'm not sure. That poncy friend of hers knows. He's the one who took the dog away.'

'Miles Quirk?'

'That's him. Bent as a nine-bob-note.'

I kept my opinion of her opinions firmly to myself and thanked her for telling me. Outside the building, I took out my phone.

'Miles?'

'Tanya? I've been trying to get a hold of you. Noreen—'

'Has gone into a hospice. Yes, a woman at her building just told me. Do you know which hospice she's in?'

'St Joseph's. Are you going to see her? I could come with you later if you like?'

'No thanks. I'm with Harry. We'll go straight there. It's important. I think she lied about what she saw the evening Vivian Blackwood was murdered.'

'You think she knows who did it.'

'I'm pretty sure.'

'Let me know what she says. I'll try to see her later today. I've got to deliver some chairs to a client. Give her my love.'

'I will.'

I got back into the van. I suppose I looked a little shellshocked.

'Where to now?' said Harry.

I looked up the postcode of the hospice on my mobile phone. After entering it into the sat-nav, we followed the cheery voice's instructions to St Joseph's, pulling up on the crunchy gravel outside the back door. I did not speak during the drive, and Harry did not ask me any questions until we got there.

'Why are we here?' he asked when he had parked the van.

'Noreen had a stroke. She's dying.'

'I'll wait in the van. Be gentle with her.'

I made my way to reception and asked if I could see Noreen Ashcroft.

'Are you family?' said the receptionist.

'No, but I'm a friend, and I wanted to get her instructions as to the care of her dog. The poor thing's been sent to a kennel, and I can only imagine the havoc. She's rather spoilt, you know. Not Noreen, her dog, Priscilla.'

The receptionist raised her eyebrow. I made puppy eyes at her.

'I know I'm babbling, but I really need to see her.'

'She's not at all well. I don't think she'll last the night. Please be brief and don't upset her, whatever you do. Ward four, bed 7, upstairs on the right.'

I thanked her and ran up the stairs to the ward. Sunlight streamed through the windows onto the beds where shrunken shells of human beings talked quietly to their families or slept with their heads thrown back. A sickly sweet smell permeated the air and made me feel nauseous. I recognised Noreen by the kaftan spread over her bed. Her hair had been brushed back off her face, and she looked as old as time. I crept over to her bed and took her hand.

'Hello Noreen. It's me, Tanya Bowe. Miles Quirk's friend.'

She screwed up her eyes to peer at my face.

'You're that detective woman, aren't you?'

'Yes, that's right.'

'Is that why you're here? About Vivian Blackwood?'

'Yes. I need to ask you some questions, if that's okay. A woman in your building told me the service lift hasn't been running at all this year. Could you have been mistaken about seeing someone using it?'

Her expression changed to one of amusement.

'Are you asking me if I was lying? I was certainly being economical with the truth.'

'Who were you protecting?'

'Who do you think? Vivian Blackwood was the scum of the earth. The person who killed him should get a medal, not a prison sentence. He saved many poor souls from blackmail and misery.'

'Are we talking about Terry Antrim?'

'Who else? DI Antrim is a proper gentleman, and he was kind to me after Bertie died. Priscilla loved him, and she's a superb judge of character.'

She grabbed my hand tighter.

'Where is she? Where's my baby?'

'They're keeping her safe in a kennel until you're better.'

'Better? I'm not getting better. Please can you ask Miles to take her? It's in my will.'

I knew Miles would rather die than adopt Priscilla, but I didn't think a dying woman needed the truth at that moment. I would think of someone mad enough to take her when my brain was not tangled in a knot.

'He'll be happy to look after her for you.'

We sat there for a moment while she gathered herself, her chest rising and falling rapidly as she fought for breath.

'Did you really see DI Antrim leave Blackwood's flat on the evening of the murder?'

'I did, but no one else.'

'So you didn't see anyone in a mac and a fedora?'

She laughed, choking on her spit. I wanted to help her sit up, but she wouldn't let me.

'Of course not. I made that up. You're not much of a detective if you believed me.'

'Did DI Antrim ask you to cover for him?'

'No, but I knew about the blackmail. Blackwood had something over DI Antrim, and he wouldn't leave it alone. Terry was desperate. Policemen earn very little you know.'

'Oh, I know. I used to be married to one.'

'Then you'll understand. The man lost his only child, for heaven's sake. It wasn't his fault. I—'

But I never found out what she would have said next. She stiffened and released a long breath, and her jaw dropped. Her eyes stayed open, but she couldn't see me anymore. Noreen Ashcroft had gone to join her husband Bertie and Mr Fluffy. I held her limp hand in mine for a little while and then laid it on the bed. I pulled the kaftan up to her chin, feeling shaken. I brushed a hair from her face.

'Happy travels, Mrs A.'

I told the nurse on duty about Noreen's demise and left the building. I sat in the van for ages trying to work through my reaction to Noreen's death. Harry sat with me, holding my hand, patient and dependable. I searched my mind for memories of Terry Antrim's visit to the Grotty Hovel when he had asked me to help him. Suddenly I realised he had meant me to catch him. Had he been afraid George might mess up? It was typical of the man that he had planned his own capture. He had planted a giant clue, which even now nestled in the pages of my notebook. I almost chuckled when I realised I had almost missed it. I guess, like George, I didn't want it to be him. Harry started the van, and we headed for the Seacastle police station.

Chapter 33

We drove straight from the hospice to the police station. I called George on my way there. A long silence followed after I told him about Terry and Noreen and the fake alibi. Finally, he sighed.

'I'll get DI Antrim to come straight here. Will you come for the interview? I'd like you to be in the room in case he disputes any of the facts.'

'Of course. I'm so sorry. I know you are fond of him. It's rather a shock.'

'No one is more shocked than I am. See you shortly.'

'Is George okay?' said Harry.

'Not really,' I said. 'I know you don't like Terry, but you must be surprised too. I never knew he had it in him.'

'Blackwood tried to ruin his career and blackmail him about the drugs he stole from lock-up for his drug-addict son. Anyone could lose their temper in those circumstances. The man isn't a saint, you know. And actually, he was growing on me.'

I kissed his cheek when we parked and squeezed his hand.

'Do you want to come in?'

Harry shook his head.

'George wouldn't like it. I'll be at the shop if you need me. I'm looking forward to a nice coffee with my brownie. Do you want to take yours with you?'

'No thanks. I'll be there soon. Keep it hidden from Ghita, though.'

He kissed me back and drove off. I stood on the pavement in front of the station feeling disoriented and miserable. Finally, I put my shoulders back and strode into the station with fake confidence. Sally Wright let me through the secure doors with no comment. I found George alone in the meeting room, his expression downcast.

'Well, this is a pretty kettle of fish,' he said. 'I never thought I'd have to accuse a fellow officer of murder. Why did Noreen Ashcroft lie about the night of the murder?'

'She was fond of Terry.'

'Weren't we all?'

We did not have to wait long for Terry to arrive. He greeted us both warmly and folded himself into a chair.

'Have you made progress with the case?' he said.

'You could say that,' said George. 'An inconsistency had come up in the evidence which you may be able to explain.'

'Go on.'

George looked at me. I flipped through to the pertinent pages of my notebook and the words blurred in front of me as I tried to read them.

'Um, yes, you, um, came to see me at home soon after the murder and asked me to help you find the killer of Vivian Blackwood. I agreed because I am your friend and I believe in you.'

'But?'

I swallowed.

'Well, you said you couldn't understand how someone could bludgeon someone to death like that. And, em…'

He shook his head.

'Ah, but how did I know that? You've got me there,' he said, smoothing his trouser legs. 'I think it's time I came clean.'

George leant forward, but he did not comment.

'On the night of the murder, I had a massive row with Vivian Blackwood who tried to blackmail me about some private information he had obtained from my phone. I would rather not discuss that information as it is not pertinent to the murder.'

'We can put it to one side for now,' said George. 'But if it becomes relevant to the case, you must tell me about it.'

'Fair enough. Anyway, I pushed him hard, and he went down. He hit his head on the floor and knocked himself out. He didn't wake immediately, so I put him in the recovery position and left him there.'

'On the floor?'

'Yes, I'm not proud of myself, but I had to get out of there before I did something worse. Anyway, I left the building, and as I was walking to my car, I received a text from him asking me to return. He apologised and said we needed to talk man-to-man and sort it out. I didn't want to go back, but I felt like I had to check on him in case he needed to go to hospital.'

'But why did you attack him? It's so unlike you,' I said.

'I didn't plan it. I lost my temper. No one is more horrified at the result than me, but the shame created by his blackmail was too great, and it turned me into a thug for a minute. I can't really explain it.'

'What happened when you went back to see Blackwood?' asked George.

'Well, the front door was open, so I let myself in. I called out, but no one answered. I went through into Blackwood's office and found him still on the floor, only, he, um, well, his um, his head had been stoved in with a stone bust. I knew he was dead, and I panicked. I ran away and left him there.'

'Why didn't you call the police?' I asked.

'Come on. You know how it would have looked. Titania already told everyone I fought with Blackwood. I was afraid of being put in prison to await trial. You know a maelstrom of pain and abuse awaits any jailed policeman, George. I was terrified I couldn't prove myself innocent. That's why I asked Tanya to help me.'

'You didn't trust me?'

'I wanted someone on my side. You had to be neutral.'

George harrumphed.

'Where was Titania when this happened?'

'I don't know. I presume she had left for the day about the same time as I arrived. I didn't notice to tell the truth. She's not someone I have warmed to.'

'Why would she leave the door open?' I said.

He shrugged.

'Maybe it was me who forgot to shut it.'

'Can you show me the text Blackwood sent you please?' said George.

Terry reached into his pocket for his mobile and scrolled through his messages. He opened the text for George to inspect.

'It's definitely from Blackwood's mobile,' said George. 'But wasn't he dead by then? Hang on, I'll get Flo.'

He picked up the internal phone and asked Flo to join us.

'Can you bring Blackwood's phone with you?' he said.

Flo did not take long to arrive. She arrived panting with exertion, her long black hair escaping from her bun.

'Sorry to keep you waiting. I had to get this from the evidence locker.'

She put the phone on the table, sealed in a plastic bag.

'Can you check the messages without damaging any fingerprints?' asked George.

'I don't think so. Are the fingerprints important? I thought it was Blackwood's phone.'

'Can you please collect them now and run them through AFIS? We'll have to get a printout of the texts from the provider. Unless anyone has the password?'

'I think Titania gave it to Mouse,' I said.

'Get him to send it to you.'

'What's going on?' asked Flo.

'What time did Blackwood die?' said George.

'I estimate seven-fourteen or later due to his watch getting damaged in the assault and stopping.'

'DI Antrim received a message sent from Blackwood's phone at seven seventeen.'

'Seven-seventeen? But he was likely dead by then.'

'That's why we want you to fingerprint the keyboard,' said George.

'I'll do it immediately,' said Flo.

'You believe me then,' said Terry.

His head sank into his hands as he exhaled with relief.

'It's not my job to believe or disbelieve anything,' said George. 'I follow the evidence. Until you told us about the message, the trail led straight to you. Now it may prove someone else killed Vivian Blackwood. I don't decide. The evidence does.'

'So who killed him then?' I said.

George smiled. He looked like Hades did when he had cornered a mouse in the kitchen.

'She's been right under our noses the entire time.'

'Titania?' I said.

'Let's get her in for questioning.'

Chapter 34

Mouse responded to my text almost immediately with Blackwood's mobile password, but we couldn't use it until Flo had lifted the fingerprints from the keyboard and logged the evidence.

'Why don't we check Blackwood's computer in the meantime to document his dealings with Titania,' I said.

'Good idea,' said George. 'I'll get Joe to take you into the secure room where it is stored. Maybe you can turn up something useful. Terry - sit tight. We haven't finished with you yet.'

I followed Joe down the passage into a small, brightly lit room where Blackwood's computer had been set up on a desk. I had mixed feelings about the fresh evidence, but I couldn't imagine how a dead man had sent a text either. George's conviction about Titania being the murderer certainly ticked all the boxes. Since Titania had been there when Mouse searched the files, I'm sure he avoided looking for evidence of her involvement. Perhaps the proof waited for us in Blackwood's files.

Joe pulled out the computer chair and let me sit in front of the keyboard.

'You type far quicker than me,' he said. 'The guv is not a patient man at the best of times.'

I waited for the console to load and logged in. The screen went blank except for a pulsating dot. Then, a bright yellow Minion appeared on screen and began to laugh and shake its rotund body. Then, it lifted a middle finger and vanished. Joe gazed at the screen open mouthed.

'What the hell?' He leant in. 'Try again,' he said.

I'm no computer geek, but I've seen the movies. Nevertheless, I tried to log in again, and again. I shook my head and let Joe try. The computer did not respond.

'Mouse's Minions,' I muttered.

'What did you say?' said Joe.

'I'm no expert, but I'd hazard a guess that someone infected Blackwood's computer with a virus. Titania belonged to a hacking group called Mouse's Minions.'

'Named after Mouse?'

'I'm afraid so. He's a cult hero in those circles. He obviously doesn't do that anymore - hacking I mean.'

'But all the evidence is gone,' said Joe. 'George will have a fit.'

'And why will I have a fit?' asked George, coming in to join us.

'The computer's fried, guv. The files are gone.'

'But Mouse told us not to connect it to the internet,' said George. 'Don't tell me you—'

'Of course not,' said Joe. 'I don't know how it happened.'

But I did.

'Titania must have done it,' I said. 'She pretended to forget her phone yesterday and ran back to get it. She was alone in the computer room for a couple of minutes.'

'That's all it takes?' said George.

'I guess she uploaded it from a USB stick. I mean, I don't know; I'm only supposing.'

'What the bloody hell do we do now?' said George, purple with rage.

'I'll call Mouse. He'll know what to do.'

Mouse answered immediately and listened patiently while I explained what had happened.

'That's definitely a virus,' he said. 'There's nothing we can do about the computer. It needs to be cleaned and rebooted. All the information is lost from there.'

'She's slipped through our fingers,' said George.

'Oh, I wouldn't say that,' said Mouse.

'What would you say?' I asked.

'Relax. I'll be there shortly. Can you ask Flo to get the copy of the hard drive out of the evidence lock-up, please?'

'The what?' said Joe.

'The copy of Blackwood's drive. The first thing I did when I accessed the files was to download a full forensic copy of Blackwood's hard drive and store it safely. Standard protocol for a forensic consultant.'

'Phew. I thought she'd caught us cold there. Thanks Mouse.'

George slapped Joe's back.

'That's my boy,' he said. 'No harm done. Can you take a couple of uniforms and pick up Titania Grafton? We'll deal with her now.'

He stomped back to his office. I suspected he needed a sugar boost after the shock of almost losing the evidence on the computer. I wandered down to Flo's lab for a chat while I waited for Mouse and Titania to turn up. I watched fascinated as she extracted the phone from the plastic bag wearing a fresh pair of gloves and placed it carefully on a paper liner on the bench. She took photographs of the keyboard from all angles and then placed the mobile into the fume cabinet.

'That's that for now. I'll lift any fingerprints shortly and compare them to the ones on file for Titania and other suspects in this case.'

'I'm so relieved Terry has been cleared,' I said.

'Not yet,' said Flo. 'What if the prints belong to him?'

'I hadn't thought of that. I'm so impressed with the care you take. London will be lucky to have you.'

She shook her head.

'I'm not joining the Met, at least not yet. They were informed about a funding freeze last week, and they can't fit me into their budget.'

'What? I can't believe it. You must be so disappointed.'

She shrugged.

'Yes, and no. I'm not sure I'm ready to test my relationship with Nick to that extent yet. I'd really like to be sure he would come with me before I accept. Being alone for so many years taught me how important it is to be loved.'

'I know exactly what you mean. I was so lucky to have found Harry. It's difficult to pick up someone like him at Sainsbury's, no matter what they say.'

I felt someone tap my shoulder. Mouse stood behind me, cracking his fingers in a display of readiness.

'Hi there, Flo. Can you please take the hard drive I gave you out of storage? I need to search for evidence of Titania's complicity with Blackwood. Joe has gone to pick her up, and George needs ammunition for the interview.'

Chapter 35

Flo and Mouse went off together, leaving me standing in the corridor. I realised the case was essentially over for me. I knocked on George's door, and he looked up from his notes.

'Are you off then?' he said. 'Thanks for your help. We couldn't have done it without you.'

'Did you have Titania down as a suspect?' I asked.

'We were planning on prosecuting her for aiding and abetting Blackwood in his blackmail scheme, but I hadn't considered her capable of murder. I guess she discovered his escape plan and realised he was about to take all their hard earned cash and make her the sacrificial lamb for her schemes. It must have been hard to take.'

'And then she found him knocked out on the floor of his office and took her revenge.'

'And framed Terry for murder. She nearly succeeded.'

'What about the Huxley sisters?'

'They were victims too. Maybe Raven will find better things to blog about.'

I doubted it. She would probably find some way of making herself the centre of the story when Titania got charged with murder. The entire case had been full of unpleasant characters from start to finish. Even the dog. And then I had a thought.

'I guess you're right. I've got to see a man about a dog.'

George grinned.

'Why do you do that here?'

'Not that sort of dog.'

I strode along the High Street to Second Home, but before I entered, I crossed the street to Surfusion where Kieron was puzzling over a menu. He looked up at me as I came in.

'I recognise that look,' he said. 'You've been plotting again.'

'Maybe. Do you remember telling me about your mother's dog?'

'Yes, the poor departed Frufru. A dreadful yappy horror, but my mother loved her.'

'What if I told you I had a replacement? A pure-bred Pomeranian who may be a demon in dog form?'

'Where can I pick it up?'

Harry welcomed me into Second Home with a lovely hug. Sometimes I think he's the psychic. How did he know I felt deflated after realising George didn't need me at the station? I had hoped to be there for the kill, but reality set in when he let me down gently. At least he had acknowledged my help with the case, something he never used to do. But even a creamy latte and a delicious brownie, squashed from being kept in Harry's pocket out of Ghita's reach, didn't take the edge off my disappointment.

'Are you going to tell me what happened?' said Harry. 'What excuses did Terry come up with? Or did George have him bang to rights? I know you like Terry, but even he can't go around murdering people just because he loses his temper.'

I laughed, despite myself.

'Oh, Terry didn't do it,' I said.

'And when were you planning on telling me?'

'Sorry. I was feeling so sorry for myself I forgot completely why I had gone to the station in the first place. It turns out Terry was framed. He didn't need Noreen's fake alibi after all.'

'Seriously? So why are you down in the dumps?'

'Because I'm a spoilt brat, I s'pose.'

He stroked my face.

'You're not a policeman. You have no right to be there except for the tolerance of George and Joe.'

'But my information was vital in solving the case. Even George admitted it.'

'But you're still not entitled to sit in on interviews. It's not like a TV show. But if it wasn't Terry who killed Blackwood; who did it?'

'Titania Grafton. At least that's what it looks like.'

'Shut up. No, she didn't. I can't believe it. You've got to tell me everything from the beginning. Don't omit anything.'

Suddenly I didn't care anymore about missing the final interview. It was easy to picture George asking a few soft questions while Titania pouted and pretended to answer them truthfully. At what stage would Flo knock on the door and present the incriminating fingerprints?

Probably right after George got Titania to claim she never used Blackwood's mobile. He would take his time explaining the timeline and let the facts sink in for themselves. And I knew Mouse would have given George and Joe a treasure trove of emails between the pair. Did he find evidence Titania knew Blackwood planned to flee with all the cash and leave her stranded? Probably. I doubted if she could bear to let them set out the facts without giving her version of events. She would dig herself a hole with steep sides from which she could not escape.

I smiled at Harry.

'Hold on to your hat,' I said.

Chapter 36

As expected, Titania could not escape the mountain of evidence presented by George and his team and ended up incarcerated at HMP Bronzefield awaiting trial for the murder of Vivian Blackwood. She had arrived full of confidence at the interview, having been convinced by Joe Brennan that the police just needed to confirm some of the evidence she had already given. She had been stunned when informed of the case against her and refused to speak any more, asking for a solicitor.

The Red Herrings would not die once the memory of them had been resurrected. Mouse ratted us out to Joy Wells of the Shanty who loved to showcase local talent. Despite our unwillingness, Joy persuaded us to take to the stage at the Shanty for one night only. As punishment, we roped Mouse and Goose into playing with us, so we were not the only ones to suffer the embarrassment of being mediocre at best. Our rehearsals took place in Second Home, upstairs in the Vintage, to the complete bemusement of the customers.

'I didn't know you played live music at the Vintage,' asked one woman. 'Are you sure Seacastle is ready for rock and roll with their lattes?'

Goose loved playing with us. His wife had had a second baby, and he took his toddler out with him to give them both a break. He had a bass guitar, which he played with solid intent. Mouse tried to be more flowery on lead guitar but ended up getting his fingers cut by the strings.

'We need the right notes, in the right order, not Jimi Hendrix at Woodstock,' said Roz.

'I'm not sure about playing the drums again,' said Ghita. 'I've lost my mojo.'

Funny enough, her mojo returned in spades when Joe Brennan popped in to watch us rehearse.

'Wow,' he said. 'Ginger Baker would be jealous.'

'Ginger who?' said Mouse.

'He drummed for Cream,' I said. 'He was a legend in his own lifetime.'

Cue frantic scrolling by Mouse and Goose.

'That's some compliment,' said Goose, looking up from his phone.

'Are you sure you don't need a hearing test?' said Mouse.

Ghita threw her drumstick at him.

'You're the one who's deaf,' she said. 'I'm pretty good at this.'

Roz and I exchanged glances. Would Ghita notice Joe being gallant or just assume she's good at everything, which, to be honest, was true? The smug look on her face told me Joe's efforts had fallen wide of the mark. I gave him a sympathetic smile. He shrugged and left again. Honestly. Ghita would keep scrubbing the floor even if Prince Charming told her she had a nice arse.

The thorny problems of what to wear and what to play entered the equation. We could not decide what would be appropriate. Roz had dug out a photograph of us as teenagers, which we had copied to use as the cover of the cassette. I stared for ages at our younger selves, wondering if we had achieved any of our dreams. Life doesn't wait while you are making plans. We were wearing outlandish costumes in the photograph. They were supposed to look like fish tails but failed. Everyone had different ideas about how we should look, but I only worried about how we would sound.

We decided to play the same songs as we had recorded for our demo tape, but we couldn't remember them all. So, Mouse finally got to rummage in Roz's attic for the cassette to make the playlist for the concert. Mouse and I went to Sarah Barrow's cottage with little hope of success, but the loft needed to be cleared in any case. Roz's mother had stuffed it full over the years. Looking for one tape in there was like searching for the proverbial needle in a haystack, but Mouse could not be dissuaded from having a go. The loft contained broken toasters, worn-out broom heads, bin bags full of old underwear and t-shirts, rails of dresses and suits decades old, and boxes full of discarded papers and books of every description. All the items were covered in dust, spiderwebs and the corpses of long-gone bluebottles.

We took the items out one by one and placed them in piles in the house's driveway. The vast majority of items were destined straight for the tip, but Roz found one or two which made her croon and hug them to her chest. These were placed on the 'take to Roz and Ed's cottage' pile. As we reached the back of the space, we found several boxes labelled 'Roz' which appeared to contain drawings and schoolbooks and photographs from Roz's early life. Mouse took these down to the lawn, and the three of us sorted through the items one by one. Roz tore the peeling parcel tape off one box and opened it with a flourish. She gasped.

'Oh my goodness. I don't believe it. Look at this.'

She held out a red sequined bolero. A logo across the back read 'Red Herrings'. She stood up and held a pair of elastic-waisted red pantaloons with sequined seams up against her legs.

'Are those what I think they are?' said Mouse.

'She never told me,' said Roz, sniffing. 'About the costumes. I thought she didn't care. She never said anything.'

Tears streamed down her cheeks as she took the rest of the costumes out of the box, shaking them out.

'Did she make them?' I asked.

'I think so,' said Roz.

'I didn't know your mother could sew.'

'Neither did I.'

'They're fantastic,' said Mouse. 'You have to wear them.'

'I'd love to, but the bottoms are far too small for me.'

'Me too,' I said, trying on a bolero. 'But this fits, and I have a pair of red velvet trousers I could wear with it.'

'Mine will still fit,' said Roz. 'Would Tanya's pantaloons fit you, Mouse?'

'Probably.'

I stifled a snort at his unwilling tone of voice.

'Ghita could wear a bolero with her red sari. It would be a fitting tribute to your mother if we finally used these outfits after so long hidden away.'

'I wish I'd known,' said Roz. 'I always thought she didn't like me much, but secretly she made us costumes. It must have taken her weeks. I'm so grateful I know about them.'

'She'll be so thrilled,' said Mouse. 'I bet she'll be watching.'

Roz hugged him tight.

'I bet she will.'

We had only a short time to prepare ourselves for the concert. We had done the bare minimum of rehearsing, practising in the shop with Mouse and Goose who both played enough electric guitar to be delusional about their talent. I have to admit I found it exhilarating and emotional to be back in a band again. I had forgotten how thrilling it could be. Harry teased me about being a rock star in his eyes, and I wallowed in nostalgia listening to the rock bands of our era. As Stephanie Coontz once said; The warm glow of nostalgia amplifies wonderful memories and minimises bad ones. I hoped Roz could make peace with the memories of her mother and find a way to remember her well.

Chapter 37

All too soon, the night of the concert arrived. I didn't feel ready, despite several last-minute practice sessions, including one at the Shanty. We had taken our instruments there and left everything set up for the concert. Joy had done a great job decorating the pub with peace signs and sparkly balloons. I couldn't believe we would actually pull it off. How on earth could I get out of singing rock songs to a crowd of disinterested teenagers and old-age pensioners? I felt like vomiting with nerves, but Harry jollied me along.

'How bad can it be?' he said. 'All your friends will be there. We'd clap if you recited the alphabet.'

The Shanty was heaving by the time Harry and I arrived. I couldn't believe how many people had turned up to hear us. Or jeer us? My legs wobbled underneath me as I walked along the path to the pub. Harry took my arm and squeezed it. I gave him a grateful peck on the cheek. The sound of glasses clinking and people laughing escaped through the windows and floated towards us as we neared the door. I took a deep breath.

Inside, Joy and Ryan had installed themselves behind the bar, which did a brisk trade.

'Maybe everyone will drink so much they won't notice how bad we are,' I said.

'You're self-sabotaging. Get a grip, trooper.'

Harry led me through to the back where Roz and Ghita had bagged our favourite table. Rohan and Kieron had joined us for the evening, and Kieron had to be restrained from adjusting our outfits.

'But you don't even match,' he said, pouting.

'We're like Culture Club, only more extreme,' I said. 'It's all the rage.'

'Nice boleros,' said Rohan. 'Very I Dream of Jeannie.'

Shaylah had brought over a tray of drinks.

'You're really going to sing,' she said. 'Rather you than me.'

'Thanks for the support,' said Roz. 'I won't bother sending you a record.'

'A record? Are you from the Stone Age?' asked Shaylah, flouncing off towards the bar.

'I think you mean CD,' said Ghita. 'Is anyone recording us? What if we're terrible?'

'I guess if we're terrible, no one will bother,' said Roz.

'Come on now,' said Harry. 'No more defeatist talk.'

'I have faith in you,' said Rohan. 'Especially in Ghita.'

She kissed him on the nose and then had to do the same to Kieron before he got jealous. Feedback issued from the speakers as Joy tapped the microphone she had grabbed from the stand. My stomach twisted into a tight knot. I told myself to relax.

'Ladies and Gentlemen,' said Joy. 'Tonight I have the infinite pleasure of presenting Seacastle's best-kept secret, reunited for one night only, by special request, featuring Mouse Carter and Goose… Oh, I don't have his actual name. Never mind. It's the one, the only, the Red Herrings!'

I don't remember walking onto the improvised stage. I turned to face the audience, and I spotted George and Helen trying to appear encouraging. Helen looked as if she might faint, although from fear or embarrassment I couldn't tell you. George grimaced into his pint. I noticed Joe Brennan staring at Ghita, eating her up with his eyes. Oh my. George clocked me looking at Joe and rolled his eyes at me. I tried not to laugh at his pained expression. I got into the mood of the evening and relaxed. Ghita slid behind the drum set and picked up the sticks. She hit the side of the drum three times and Mouse and Goose played the first chords of Hotel California.

We had fumbled the intro, but that didn't seem to matter to the audience. As I started singing, it occurred to me that Seacastle and Hotel California had a lot in common. Maybe Flo wouldn't be able to leave either. The thought relaxed me even more, and I heard myself singing like a pro. Not to be outdone Roz came in with the harmonies, and we were off. The audience responded to our obvious enjoyment by belting out the hits with us. I've never been at one with an audience before, and I'm sure I won't be again, but something magical happened that night at the Shanty. Something special. People came up to me in the street for months afterwards to praise the show. I'll never forget it.

As we were bowing at the end of our set, Ghita came out from behind the drums and took the microphone off the stand. She stood quietly waiting for the hubbub to die down with a strange look on her face — a short plump woman with a sparkly bolero and a bright red sari. Eventually, people realised she was waiting to speak and stopped talking. She took a deep breath and stood on her tiptoes.

'I have an announcement to make,' she said. 'I am running for the council seat left empty by Craig Latchford. I've worked at the council for years in the engine room, and now I'd like to be the face of Seacastle. It's time we had someone representing the town who isn't lining their pockets!'

After an astonished silence, loud cheering broke out. Mouse started a chant of 'Ghita, Ghita' but soon gave up. Ghita smiled.

'I hope you will all vote for me. I'll not betray your trust. Thank you.'

I gazed at her in amazement. I don't think I've ever been so proud of her. Then we enveloped her in a group hug with Roz and Mouse. Goose stood to one side, looking awkward, holding both guitars and grinning.

'You'll be brilliant,' I said. 'They won't know what's hit them.'

Joe Brennan approached us and took advantage of the excitement to give Ghita a hug too. She turned bright crimson, matching her sari exactly. Roz winked at me, and I knew she had noticed too.

Ryan came over with a tray of drinks balanced on his wheelchair's special attachment.

'On the house,' he said. 'Maybe you could do a residency?'

'Absolutely not,' I said. 'One night only means only one night.'

'I'm running for councillor,' said Ghita. 'I can't get involved in drink and drugs right now.'

'I'd soon be a lush if I spent all my time in the Shanty,' said Roz.

'I made a recording of the show. I'm going to give you all a CD each as a memento. Can I sell copies for charity at the bar?'

'Of course,' I said. 'As long as the others don't mind.'

'Count me in,' said Roz.

'You could call them the Pickled Herrings if they drink too much tonight,' said Kieron.

'The Sozzled Sisters,' said Harry.

'You can call me Councillor,' said Ghita. 'If I win.'

'When you win,' I said. 'I'm going outside for a minute to cool down.'

Actually, I just wanted to stargaze, but Harry immediately put his jacket around my shoulders.

'We'll be back,' he said.

'A likely story,' said Roz. 'You're going out for a snog.'

We ignored her and left through the absurdly small entrance door, crouching to avoid hitting our heads. Outside, the moon hung in the sky like a forgotten Christmas bauble. For once, the stars outshone the streetlights. I breathed in deeply.

'You were brilliant,' said Harry. 'I had no idea you could sing like that.'

'Neither did I. It just happened. Did you notice the way Joe Brennan looks at Ghita? I think he's fallen for her.'

Harry grinned. 'It's about time someone did.'

'Does she know?'

'She's oblivious.'

'And how do you know?'

'Roz.'

'She's feeling better, then.'

'So it seems.'

He leant down and kissed the top of my head.

I looked out over the sea, the town lit up behind us and allowed myself to dream a little.

Chapter 38

The gentle heat generated by the early summer sunshine soon made me take off my coat and fling it over my shoulder. The tide had gone out, and the rock pools had growths of bright green algae, which made the beach look like a lumpy water-meadow. The wind farm gleamed in the distance, its turbines turning in the constant breeze of the English Channel. I stopped to take a couple of deep breaths in the wind shelter and meditated on the death of Vivian Blackwood.

I could not raise any sympathy in my heart about his murder. He deserved it. His complete lack of empathy with his lonely and often desperate clients had shocked me to the core. I couldn't help feeling Titania had done the world a favour. I secretly applauded her for it. Joe Brennan definitely sympathised with this point of view, but I doubted George felt the same way. His black-and-white worldview did not allow sympathy for the devil. Titania would go to prison for years, not as long as for a pre-planned murder, but long enough to grow older in there. I wondered if being locked up would change her or if she would remain convinced that she was the actual victim of Blackwood's crimes.

Helen told me George had been incredibly relieved when Terry was exonerated. He could not compute the possibility DI Antrim had murdered a fellow human. I fully understood his attacking Blackwood. If anyone tried to harm Harry or Mouse or anyone I loved, I could not be sure I wouldn't have done the same in his position. George would arrest them, of course. I suspect Harry would call his pals in the SAS. No messing about there. Everyone thinks they couldn't murder someone. I bet Titania thought that before it happened. But it had. Water under the bridge. I tried to forget about Titania Grafton and enjoy the view instead.

Harry arrived carrying our breakfast in a plastic bag and holding a large flask of tea. He took out the bacon sandwiches and handed me one.

'Ketchup and brown bread,' he said. 'As madam requested.'

He took his own sandwich out. Brown sauce and white bread, if you're curious. We ate in companionable silence as the waves rolled the pebbles on the bank slowly wearing away their sharp edges. A loud flapping noise signalled the arrival of Hector with his massive wingspan. He flopped onto his pink webbed feet and tilted his head at us.

'How does he know?' said Harry. 'He must have radar or something.'

'Can seagulls smell bacon? Maybe he saw you with the plastic bag. They're clever birds. Have you seen that video of one stealing a bag of crisps from a shop?'

'You spend far too much time on your phone.'

'It's Mouse's fault.'

'No, it isn't. He's not forcing you to doom-scroll all the time. But he should never have made you get a smartphone. You have an addictive personality.'

'No, I haven't. I get bored easily. TikTok was invented for people like me with short attention spans.'

'Are you admitting you're a goldfish?'

'At least I don't watch hours and hours of cricket. That's just as bad.'

'It's not the same. Cricket is a sport.'

'Mouse says doomscrolling will be a sport in the Los Angeles Olympics.'

Harry laughed.

'He's pulling your leg.'

Hector squawked loudly and padded forward with his beak open.

'I nearly forgot to save him the crusts.'

'He might try eating us one of these days. I swear he's still growing.'

'He has his chicks to feed.'

'It's a serious job being a father.'

Harry stroked my face.

'I'm serious about the baby, you know.'

The lump in my throat stopped me from replying. I leant against him and watched the waves.

'Do you think a child of ours would like antiques?' I said.

Thank you for reading Malign Fortune. Please leave me a review if you enjoyed it.

Loved *Malign Fortune*? Don't miss Tanya's next case! Pre-order Poison Politics on Amazon and join Tanya as she searches for the spider in a political web.

Other books

Other books in the Seacastle Mysteries - a cosy mystery series set on the south coast of England

Deadly Return (Book 1)
Staying away is hard, but returning may prove fatal.
Tanya Bowe, a former investigative journalist, is adjusting to life as an impoverished divorcee in the seaside town of Seacastle. She crosses paths with a long-lost schoolmate, Melanie Conrad, during a house clearance to find stock for her vintage shop. The two women renew their friendship, but their reunion takes a tragic turn when Mel is found lifeless at the foot of the stairs in the same house.

While the police are quick to label Mel's death as an accident, Tanya's gut tells her there's more to the story. Driven by her instincts, she embarks on her own investigation, delving into Mel's mysterious past. As she probes deep into the Conrad family's secrets, Tanya uncovers a complex web of lies and blackmail. But the further she digs, the more intricate the puzzle becomes. As Tanya's determination grows, so does the shadow of danger. Each new revelation brings her closer to a chilling truth. Can she unravel the secrets surrounding Mel's demise before the killer strikes again?
Eternal Forest (Book 2)

What if proving a friend's husband innocent of murder implicates her instead?

Tanya Bowe, an ex-investigative journalist and divorcee, runs a vintage shop in the coastal town of Seacastle. When her old friend, Lexi Burlington-Smythe borrows the office above the shop as a base for the campaign to create a kelp sanctuary off the coast, Tanya is thrilled with the chance to get involved and make some extra money. Tanya soon gets drawn into the high-stake arguments surrounding the campaign, as tempers are frayed, and her friends, Roz and Ghita favour opposing camps. When a celebrity eco warrior is murdered, the evidence implicates Roz's husband Ed, and Tanya finds her loyalties stretched to breaking point as she struggles to discover the true identity of the murderer.

Fatal Tribute (Book 3)

How do you find the murderer when every act is convincing?

Tanya Bowe, an ex-investigative journalist, agrees to interview the contestants of the National Talent Competition for the local newspaper, but finds herself up to her neck in secrets, sabotage and simmering resentment. The tensions increase when her condescending sister comes to stay next door for the duration of the contest.

Several rising stars on the circuit hope to win the competition, but old stager, Lance Emerald, is not going down without a fight. When Lance is found dead in his dressing room, Tanya is determined to find the murderer, but complex dynamics between the contestants and fraught family relationships make the mystery harder to solve. Can Tanya uncover the truth before another murder takes centre stage?

Toxic Vows (Book 4)

A shotgun marriage can lead to deadly celebrations

Despite her reservations, Tanya Bowe, ex-investigative journalist and local sleuth, feels obliged to plan and attend the wedding of her ex-husband DI George Carter. The atmosphere is less than convivial as underlying tensions bubble to the surface. But when the bride is found dead only hours after the ceremony, the spotlight is firmly turned onto George as the prime suspect. A reluctant Tanya is forced to come to George's aid when his rival, DI Antrim is determined to prove him responsible for her death. She discovers the bride had a lot of dangerous secrets, but so did other guests at the wedding. Did the murderer intend to kill, or has an elaborate plan gone badly wrong?

Mortal Vintage (Book 5)

Does an ancient coven hold the key to solving a murder?

Few tears are shed when the unpopular manager of the annual Seacastle Vintage Fair meets a sinister end. But local sleuth Tanya Bowe is thrust into the heart of the investigation when her friend, Grace Wong, finds herself under scrutiny for the murder. When Tanya's investigation uncovers a suspicious death in the same family, all bets are off. She navigates dark undercurrents of greed and betrayal as she uncovers a labyrinth of potential suspects associated with an ancient coven. Nothing is as it seems, and every clue adds extra complications. To solve the case, Tanya must answer one key question. Did someone hate the victim enough to kill her, or was greed the stronger motive?

Last Orders (Book 6)

Has a restaurant critic's scathing review led to his murder?

The grand opening of the Surfusion restaurant attracts a famous food critic, raising the stakes for the owners.

The night takes a dark turn when he collapses into his coffee, hours after his scathing review goes live. Local sleuth Tanya Bowe, a friend of the owners, witnesses the shocking incident and vows to clear their names.

As Tanya digs deeper, what at first seems like an open-and-shut case against the owners unravels into a web of intrigue. Is the famous critic even the intended victim of the crime? Tanya Bowe has her work cut out for her as hidden motives lead to simmering tensions among her friends. With time running out and Surfusion's future on the line, can Tanya unmask the culprit before it's too late?

Grave Reality (Book 7)
A reality show turns deadly when death rewrites the script.
Chaos breaks out in the quiet town of Seacastle when the cast and crew of the hit show Sloane Rangers descend upon it, stirring up drama both on and off the screen. Local sleuth and former investigative reporter, Tanya Bowe, is brought on board as a consultant, tasked with recommending perfect filming locations for the episode. Tanya soon uncovers a tangled web of strained relationships and simmering tensions among the cast members. When one of the stars of the show is discovered unconscious in her room, Tanya finds herself at the heart of a complex murder investigation where everyone is a suspect. Unravelling the truth seems impossible when many of them have difficulty distinguishing real life from the scripted show. As the case unfolds, several beloved cast members emerge as the prime suspects, sending shockwaves through Seacastle. With everyone playing a part and secrets buried deep, the murderer remains hidden in plain sight. Can Tanya unravel the truth before someone else dies?

Lethal Secret (Book 8)

When one woman is murdered and another vanishes, an investigation uncovers a wartime mystery—and a killer with unfinished business.

The Shanty pub is the heart of Seacastle—a place for laughter, friendship, and the occasional small-town drama. But when a woman is found dead outside, the town is left reeling—especially when the victim bears a striking resemblance to Joy Wells, the pub's co-owner, who hasn't returned from a trip to Budapest. To the people of Seacastle, Joy and her husband, Ryan, are just the couple who run the pub. But Joy and Ryan have secret lives—and someone from their past may be back for revenge. With Ryan growing desperate and the police getting nowhere, Tanya sets out to find Joy herself. Following a trail that leads from the Sussex coast to the streets of Budapest, she uncovers more questions than answers. What was Joy really doing abroad? Why did someone want her gone? And how far will they go to settle old scores? But time is running out, and every step closer to the truth raises the stakes. Will Tanya find Joy before she disappears for good?

Poison Politics (Book 10)

When a council auditor drops dead after a routine meeting, Seacastle is rocked by whispers of poison, corruption…and murder. Tanya Bowe is certain the truth lies somewhere between the buffet table and the ballot box. But with her friend Ghita launching a campaign to unseat the shameless Craig Latchford, the timing couldn't be worse. The opposition is already throwing mud—and some of it is sticking. As rumours of dodgy contracts and backroom deals spread, Tanya is drawn into a tangle of suspects: slippery contractors, ambitious councillors, and more than one person with a reason to silence the victim. To make matters worse, Raven Huxley is back in town—claiming to "help" Ghita while stirring mischief at every turn. With an election looming, a killer on the loose, and Seacastle's reputation on the line, Tanya must dig deep into her reporter's instincts to expose the truth. Can she untangle the lies before another life is lost—and before Ghita's political career is poisoned for good?

Purrfect Crime – A Seacastle Christmas Novella
The purrfect Christmas mystery to keep you up all night.
When preparations for Christmas at the Grotty Hovel are interrupted by the discovery of a body in the back garden, local sleuth, Tanya Bowe, finds herself embroiled in a cold case mystery. The local police are less than enthusiastic about pursuing the case before the holidays, but Tanya can't wait. Then Hades, their rescue cat, goes missing, and all festivities are put on hold as Tanya and her housemates search high and low for their pesky feline. As the hunt for Hades becomes more frantic, Tanya suspects his disappearance may be linked to the body in her garden. Who has kit-napped Hades? Will Tanya find the murderer before the turkey starts to rot?

Box Sets

Seacastle Mysteries Boxset Volumes 1-4
Seacastle Mysteries Boxset volumes 5-8

OTHER BOOKS BY THE AUTHOR

I write under various pen names in different genres. If you are looking for another mystery, why don't you try Mortal Mission, written as Pip Skinner.

Mortal Mission

Will they find life on Mars, or death?

When the science officer for the first crewed mission to Mars dies suddenly, backup Hattie Fredericks gets the coveted place on the crew. But her presence on the Starship provokes suspicion when it coincides with a series of incidents that threaten to derail the mission.

After a near-miss while landing on the planet, the world watches as Hattie and her fellow astronauts struggle to survive. But, worse than the harsh elements on Mars, is their growing realisation that someone, somewhere, is trying to destroy the mission.

When more astronauts die, Hattie doesn't know who to trust. And her only allies are 35 million miles away. As the tension ratchets up, violence and suspicion invade both worlds. If you like science-based sci-fi and a locked-room mystery with a twist, you'll love this book.

The Green Family Saga

Rebel Green – Book 1

Relationships fracture when two families find themselves caught up in the Irish Troubles.

The Green family moves to Kilkenny from England in 1969, at the beginning of the conflict in Northern Ireland. They rent a farmhouse on the outskirts of town and make friends with the O'Connor family next door.

Not every member of the family adapts easily to their new life, and their differing approaches lead to misunderstandings and friction. Despite this, the bonds between the family members deepen with time.

Perturbed by the worsening violence in the North threatening to invade their lives, the children make a pact never to let the troubles come between them. But promises can be broken, with tragic consequences for everyone.

Africa Green – Book 2

Will a white chimp save its rescuers or get them killed?

Journalist Isabella Green travels to Sierra Leone, a country emerging from civil war, to write an article about a chimp sanctuary. Animals that need saving are her obsession, and she can't resist getting involved with the project, which is on the verge of bankruptcy. She forms a bond with local boy, Ten, and army veteran, Pete, to try to save it. When they rescue a rare white chimp from a village frequented by a dangerous rebel splinter group, the resulting media interest could save the sanctuary. But the rebel group has not signed the ceasefire. They believe the voodoo power of the white chimp protects them from bullets, and they are determined to take it back so they can storm the capital. When Pete and Ten go missing, only Isabella stands in the rebels' way. Her love for the chimps unlocks the fighting spirit within her. Can she save the sanctuary, or will she die trying?

Fighting Green – Book 3

Liz Green is desperate for a change. The dot-com boom is raging in the City of London, and she feels exhausted and out of her depth. Added to that, her long-term boyfriend, Sean O'Connor, is drinking too much and shows signs of going off the rails. Determined to start anew, Liz abandons both Sean and her job, and buys a near-derelict house in Ireland to renovate.

She moves to Thomastown where she renews old ties and makes new ones, including two lawyers who become rivals for her affection. When Sean's attempt to win her back goes disastrously wrong, Liz finishes with him for good. Finding herself almost penniless, and forced to seek new ways to survive, Liz is torn between making a fresh start and going back to her old loves.

Can Liz make a go of her new life, or will her past become her future?

Sam Harris Adventure Series

If you fancy gripping adventures incorporating real-life incidents from the author's career, you will love The Sam Harris Adventure Series (written as PJ Skinner)

Set in the late 1980s and through the 1990s, the thrilling Sam Harris Adventure series navigates through the career of a female geologist. Themes such as women working in formerly male domains, and what constitutes a normal existence, are developed in the context of Sam's constant ability to find herself in the middle of an adventure or mystery. Sam's home life provides a contrast to her adventures and feeds her need to escape. Her attachment to an unfaithful boyfriend is the thread running through her romantic life, and her attempts to break free of it provide another side to her character.

The first book in the Sam Harris Series sets the scene for the career of an unwilling heroine, whose bravery and resourcefulness are needed to navigate a series of adventures set in remote sites in Africa and

South America. Based loosely on the real-life adventures of the author, the settings and characters are given an authenticity that will connect with readers who enjoy adventure fiction and mysteries set in remote settings with realistic scenarios.

Connect with the Author

PJ Skinner was born in Guildford, one of seven siblings. When she was six, the family moved to Ireland where she attended school. She went to Trinity College, Dublin University, graduating as a geologist. After graduation, PJ spent 35 years working in over thirty countries as an exploration geologist. PJ worked in many remote, strange, and often dangerous places, and loved every minute, despite encountering her fair share of misogyny and other perils. During this time, she collected the tall tales and real-life experiences which inspired her to write the Sam Harris Adventure Series. The series chronicles the adventures of a pioneering female geologist in an almost exclusively male world.

After finishing the Sam Harris Adventure series, PJ's childhood in Ireland inspired her to write the Green Family Saga, which follows the fortunes of an English family who move to Ireland just before the start of the Troubles, under the name of Kate Foley.

PJ moved to the south coast of England just before the Covid pandemic. There she wrote Mortal Mission, a sci-fi mystery set on Mars, inspired by her fascination with all things celestial. It is a science-based murder mystery; think The Martian with fewer potatoes and more bodies.

The enjoyment of writing Mortal Mission encouraged her to try writing a mystery series. She has always been a massive fan of crime and mystery, so it was inevitable she would turn her hand to it eventually. She published Deadly Return, the first book in the Seacastle Mysteries in July 2023 to great success. The Seacastle Mystery Series is a contemporary cosy mystery series with an amateur female sleuth, her grumpy ex-husband, hacker stepson and ungrateful rescue cat. The ensemble cast adds banter and humour as the series follows their stories between the murder mysteries. Malign Fortune, book 9, was released on the 31st of August 2025.

Please subscribe to the Seacastle Mysteries Newsletter for updates and offers through this link.

You can also use the QR code below to get to the website for updates and to buy paperbacks and PJ Skinner Merch direct from her.

You can also follow her on Twitter, Instagram, TikTok, or on Facebook @pjskinnerauthor

www.ingramcontent.com/pod-product-compliance
Lightning Source LLC
Chambersburg PA
CBHW050603190726
48283CB00007B/2257